Love on Top

Cheryl Barton

Published by: CRBarton Productions

CRBarton Productions, LLC
P.O. Box 962
Reisterstown, Maryland 21136
www.crbarton.com

Ordering Information:
Quantity sales. Special discounts are available on quantity purchases by corporations, associations, and others. For details, contact the publisher at the address above.

Orders by U.S. trade bookstores and wholesalers. Please contact prez@crbarton.com

ISBN: 0-9978779-5-2
ISBN-13: 978-0-9978779-5-3

Love on Top

I'm back at it again and I have to say I enjoyed telling Brandon and Dakota King's story. We hear a lot about people giving up too easy on marriage and not fighting for what they once had. I want readers to know that a love worth getting is one worth having and keeping. Brandon may have been slow in understanding that, but as long as there is a chance, it's never too late to put love on top of everything else!

Happy Reading!

Cheryl

1~Love on Top

The minute Dakota heard the phone ringing throughout the house and she knew it was already pretty late in the evening, the only person calling this late had to be Brandon calling with another story or excuse to try and explain another late, late night working. Despite how relaxing her day had been, she could feel frustration creeping up her spine. Her first inkling was to let it ring and not answer, but she knew if it was him, he'd get anxious knowing she was at home with their kids alone. After getting no response, knowing Brandon the way she did, he would continue calling between the house phone and her cell phone until he got an answer and if still nothing, he'd come flying through the door, worried at first and then angry that she'd made him terrified with thoughts that something bad could have happened to them.

Maybe he needed to worry more if that meant he'd come home. Despite how angry she was at his increasing number of extended absences lately, she didn't want to put him through the unnecessary angst that something could be wrong at home.

With as much attitude as she could muster up, she snatched up the house phone from the nightstand before it stopped ringing.

"What is it this time, Brandon?" she said before giving him a chance to say hello. The patience she typically tried to maintain when it came to him had flown out the door weeks ago when the excuses for his absence around the house started to become the norm.

When she married him eight years ago, a year after graduating from college, she never expected to get to a day when she'd start feeling like a single parent raising their children by herself. Even the kids started noticing his absence and were asking for him more than they ever have before. Each time she made up an excuse for him not being around, she saw the look of disappointment on their faces. She could handle being disappointed by Brandon, though it still bothered her, but she wasn't going to continue to accept what it was doing to their children. Jasmine at seven and Braden at four should expect to have both of their parents actively involved in their lives on a daily basis.

"I can't get a hello before you give me attitude and go nuclear?" Brandon asked.

It didn't escape her that he was trying to keep the mood light knowing that unless he was calling to say he was on his way, the conversation wasn't going to go well.

"When you're calling this late at night for the fourth time this week and we're only five days in and I suspect I know the reason for this call, I'm not in the mood for dishing out hellos. I assume this is another call about something important or some emergency again at the club or at the construction site and I shouldn't expect you anytime soon. Am I in the ballpark?" she asked with enough irritation in her voice to make sure her frustration with him was crystal clear.

Hearing Brandon huff on the other end of the phone angered her more. What did he have to be upset about? He was living the life having his home life taken care of and in perfect condition whenever he decided to come home and spend time with his wife and children. If she didn't know any better, she'd think that he was cheating on her. All the signs were there – his being gone all the time, especially after hours, his disinterest in anything family related and their lack of intimacy over the past few months. Brandon's appetite for sex was voracious and had been since the first time they'd made love when they were in college. She loved how even after years of marriage, he couldn't seem to get enough of her, until lately that is, but something in their love life had changed and she was worried.

"You know what I'm trying to do and it's all about business, so I don't get why I receive disdain and anger from you. Everything I do, I do for you and the kids and you know that. Without everything I'm doing, we wouldn't have the life we're living, so a little more support from you would be appreciated," he said curtly.

Hearing his tone, the conversation was headed down the same path that it always seemed to go and it wasn't a happy one.

Dakota had to hold the phone out and look it over to be sure she heard what she thought she heard. For an instant, she had a premise that her husband had lost his mind. She was nothing but supportive and had been since the day they'd met. She was the dutiful wife maintaining the home, taking care of the kids and helping out with his businesses whenever he needed her. What she didn't support or sign up for was a husband who spent more time away from home than in it. She wanted more of Brandon, more of the man she married eight years ago who made her a priority in his life. She no longer felt like she was in that position and it bothered her.

"Don't talk to me like I don't support you every day with everything you do. I am your biggest supporter despite the fact that I see less and less of you with every passing day. I deserve just as much time as your business ventures. As soon as I think it's getting better and you've reached an achievement, you start something new and you're away more and more. I thought tonight we were going to have a family night and the kids were looking forward to it. Every time lights passed down our street, they would look toward the garage to see if they could hear you pulling in. We don't usually get a lot of traffic because there are only four houses in our secluded development, but it seemed like a major highway of traffic tonight, the one night they were really looking forward to time alone with you. When they finally fell asleep in the family room, I put them to bed and knew that I shouldn't even think about waiting up for you. If you're calling about another late night, save it. I guess there's no need in waiting up."

"Dakota, aren't you tired of fighting with me all the time about the same thing? I'm sorry about tonight, but it couldn't be avoided."

"Of course not. I have no doubt it couldn't be avoided because nothing around here is as much a priority as your latest money-making endeavor, right?"

Dakota sat up in bed, bracing for an intense discussion because there was no way she was going to let him sugarcoat his lack of time and attention to his family.

"That's not fair and you know it," he said.

"Really? Not fair? What is really going on, Brandon? Is it really work that's taking up your time or something else? Is it another woman?

Women? All these late nights, it can't always be work. You're gone all day starting the moment the sun comes up and then all evening and well into the night. You come home long enough to change and remind us that you are still a part of this family and then you're gone again. You make plans with me and the kids and then you cancel with one excuse after another. What happened to the family trip we were going to take before the kids start school in a few weeks? They only have a little over a month left before the first day of school and we had planned to take them to Disney World, to the beach, to other amusement parks and instead, I end up taking them someplace to make up for the fact that you've found something more important to you than your family," she pleaded with exasperation.

"It's midnight, Dakota and I don't want to get into this with you again and again. I don't have to call and tell you I'm going to be late like I have to check-in; I'm doing it because it's the right thing to do, but if you're going to get all crazy about it every time, then I won't do it at all," he countered angrily.

"Seriously, if you think you're doing me a favor by calling me late night to say you'll be home sometime before the sun comes up, save yourself the breath. I preferred the days of the past when you would call this late at night for a booty call, but I guess getting married and having kids, you no longer feel that's a necessity, you know, that thing called paying attention to your wife. Hey, you consider it an imposition to do anything but work these days, so you do that. I've had enough excuses to last me a lifetime."

"Well, I miss having a wife who understands the importance of what I'm doing. Where is that woman?"

Dakota's anger now boiled over.

"You know where she is? She's at home in bed alone for another night wondering if her husband has found another bed to warm at night because it's clear it's not the one at the house where he lives. She's here taking care of your house and your children, making sure that despite having an absentee father, they are still happy and thriving. She's here being everything you need when you need it and she has a right to question when providing needs is no longer a two-way street. You know what? I am tired of fighting Brandon, so screw you and good night."

Before he could respond, Dakota hung up and then unplugged the phone. She didn't even want to be tempted to answer if he called back.

After turning out the light on the nightstand, she rolled over and tried to focus on anything that would help her fall asleep since she was amped up after another nasty fight.

Her mind took her back to happier times before and right after they married.

She'd met Brandon through his sister, Alisha, who she had been best friends with since their freshman year in college at Norfolk State in Virginia. Brandon, their brother Aiden and their parents had come to the school to support Alisha for her first time on the field as a dancing majorette. After the game, Alisha introduced her to the family and there were sparks between her and Brandon that couldn't be denied. From that day, they were inseparable. Brandon and Aiden, who were twins, were juniors in college at Howard University and as often as he could get away, he would drive down to Norfolk on weekends and they would hang out. Those weekends helped make her first time being away from home enjoyable.

Brandon was unlike most of the guys she knew back at home in Philadelphia where she had been born and raised. Most didn't have dreams beyond getting out of high school, but Brandon knew he was going to make something big out of life and he was making plans to achieve that even while still in school. She loved that his plans included big dreams with major successes and also included a life with her.

In her sophomore year, her father was able to buy her a used car and once she and Alisha were on the road, all of their spare time was spent between Howard and Norfolk and they ended up being more like sisters than just college roommates. They not only took road trips to Howard University, but they would drive to Baltimore where Alisha was from and she'd show her around town.

After graduating college, with Brandon and Aiden already using their degrees in Business Management and opening up their first night club together, Dakota was surprised when Brandon proposed to her in front of her family at her college graduation party. His family was also in attendance and other than the day they'd met, it was the happiest day of her life. From there, life was a big rollercoaster ride. She'd planned their wedding which was the kind little girls dreamed about. A year later, they welcomed their first child and she'd never looked back until lately.

She and Brandon agreed early that as long as they could afford it, she would stay home until the kids were old enough to be in school all day. She didn't mind because she loved bonding and spending time with the kids, time she'd never get back if they were in daycare all day while she worked. Her degree in Accounting could take her in many directions eventually and she didn't have a problem waiting until her kids were older to dive into the working world.

Brandon provided a great life for them. After their wedding, she moved to Miami where he and Aiden had moved to open their first club. That club instantly became the hottest spot in the Miami Beach area, a favorite of celebrities around the world. With the success of that club, they opened up several supper clubs and three other popular restaurants and bars inside of three five-star hotels.

Business was booming, but in the midst of all of that success, their home life began to suffer, especially when they decided to open a second location for their nightclub. Due to the popularity of the first one, they often maxed out on the number of patrons early in the night and knew it was time to expand. That expansion had led to long days and nights of Brandon being away from her and the children.

By now, she thought life would be different and once Brandon and Aiden were successful, they would hire the people they needed to run their businesses and she would get her husband back, giving them more family time before the kids got too big to appreciate having experiences of vacations that some kids never get to experience. Most didn't because of a lack of money, but she never imagined her kids wouldn't because of the lack of a parent being around.

Dakota tossed around on the bed and turned back to face her nightstand where a picture of her and Brandon sat. It was a picture taken on the island of Jamaica where they went for their honeymoon and it was where they made commitments to each other to always place family first and to always put their love first. She'd done everything to make that happen and yet she felt like their love was slipping away.

She tried going to where he was in order to spend time with him, but times where she would go to the club, Brandon was so busy running things that he didn't have time to have a drink or even dance with her. She understood he had a business to run, but there were times when that was the only time that she got to see him. She hated thinking of the conversations she'd overhear of women talking about him and all the things they like to do to him. She'd watch them flaunt shamelessly in front of him and he appeared to be sucking up all that attention. He told her that it was all a part of the business and it's only successful if people enjoyed being in the club. Still, knowing the things these women were willing to do just to get closer to him, she wondered how much declining a man could actually do before he indulged, especially when his wife and children were safely tucked away at home.

After having two children, she wasn't sure she was still as sexy to him as some of the young hot women in little black dresses he encountered nightly and those type of thoughts began to play havoc with her mind. Nothing she did seemed to interest him or perhaps, as Alisha said to her, it was all in her mind.

During one of their outings, she'd told Alisha about her reservations about pending problems in her marriage and Alisha brushed it off and told her that Brandon had loved her since the first moment she'd introduced them and that she had nothing to worry about. Still, something was wrong and she didn't know how to fix it. They were growing apart and she didn't know how to bridge the gap.

Thinking of what could be happening to her marriage caused her eyes to mist over and a tear fell down her cheek and onto the pillow. As she laid in bed alone, something she has been doing a lot of lately, her mind couldn't help, but wander to the possibility that Brandon had tired of her and had moved on to someone else, someone younger, sexier, hotter and not married to him. That caused her to cry even harder until sleep took over.

2-Love on Top

Brandon walked into his house quietly to keep from waking Dakota and the kids. It was four in the morning and he'd finally been able to get away from the club after closing and then spending another hour going over some changes in the plans for the layout of the new club. It was the best time to get it done since Aiden was there along with their building developer who was in town from Atlanta. He knew how busy Duron Knight was and he was glad that after their meeting earlier in the day at the construction site, that he'd stuck around to enjoy an evening at the club.

Duron's architectural firm, Pioneer Architecture & Design, was one of the fastest growing in the country, based out of Atlanta, Georgia with other locations in California and a new one he and his partners, Michael Bailey and Tyrone Davis, had opened in Texas. They were under contract for the design and build of the new nightclub on land he was able to acquire after many discussions with the city of Miami.

Duron was scheduled to fly out early in the morning, so they decided to have a quick meeting at the end of the night. He could respect a man who couldn't wait to get out of town and get back home to his wife Taija and their children, a set of rambunctious twins, according to him. A round of congratulations went out when Duron told them that his wife was pregnant with their third child. Laughter ensued when everyone questioned if she was pregnant with twins again. Duron feigned a heart attack and said they confirmed early that she was only carrying one this time.

Hearing Duron talk about his wife and kids had him thinking of his own wife and children at home and the argument he'd had with Dakota just a few hours before. They had been arguing a lot lately, but in his heart, he knew that he was making all of his moves to be sure they would be taken care of. He and Aiden were in the middle of construction of what he knew would be the hottest spot in Miami only besting the spot at the top that was currently held by his first club and there was a lot to be done. He knew he wasn't being the husband and father he needed to be, but he told himself it was only temporary if he could get her to understand what he was up against and how big this new project was.

The new club was three times the size of the current club and would have three levels where they were planning to have a live band on the top floor. They were also planning to have a large outside patio right on the beach, providing them with a fourth dance floor besides the ones on each level of the club.

The supper clubs were booming, the bars and restaurants in the hotels were doing better than ever. He and Aiden were set to have a meeting in a few weeks to expand and open a club in New York and one Los Angeles, which was going to be major for them. That could possibly mean more time away from Dakota and the kids and it would mean travel that could take him away for days or weeks at a time, something he knew wouldn't go over well with her, which is why he hadn't told her about those new undertakings yet. In due time, he thought, when she wasn't as angry as she had been when he called her earlier to say he'd be late.

Lately they hadn't been getting along and every time they had a discussion, it turned into a heated dispute. He knew he needed to do better, but they wouldn't survive if he didn't push harder and work for more in the competitive night club world. He was hoping that by the end of the summer, he'd get some time to take the family away for a few trips, but it wasn't looking like he was going to be able to hold up his end of the bargain, especially with the possibility of the deals to expand to other cities. He wanted Dakota to be happy for all of the success he was achieving, but she was far from happy about anything these days. She rarely smiled, except when it came to the kids. If she was upset, angry or depressed about anything, she never let the kids see her that way and he appreciated that. There was no need for their children to get caught up in the middle of their issues. They needed to find a way to work them out.

Walking through the quiet house, he knew they were asleep and he saw remnants of them having a fun night in the family room. Even though he was exhausted, he took the time to straighten up and put the toys away that had been laying around. When he went to pick up the papers and crayons from the table in the middle of the room, he picked up a drawing that was most likely Braden's because Jasmine was much better at drawing. In the picture, Braden had drawn a picture of them as a family, though what he looked at disturbed him. It was a picture he had drawn of the house and inside was him, Jasmine and Dakota, but Brandon didn't see himself in that part of the picture. On the other side was a picture of a man working on a building with a ladder and tool belt and under it he'd written the words, 'Daddy working'. The words that Dakota spoke to him all the time, were now ringing true with his son and that wasn't good. He picked up the picture and tucked it inside of his laptop case before heading upstairs to the bedroom.

Making sure the alarm was set and all the lights were off, he went up, not sure if Dakota would be awake or asleep. If she heard him come in, she may be up and they would end up engaging in another heated argument, especially with the hour in which he was once again coming home.

Going first to check on the kids, he smiled seeing them peacefully asleep and when he went into Braden's room to tuck him back up under the covers, he smiled at how wildly his son slept when he saw that the blanket was half on him and half on the bed along with part of Braden's body. One big toss and he'd be on the floor. Luckily, he liked sleeping on the bottom bunk of his bed and it wasn't a huge drop to the floor in case he fell off. Giving him a quick kiss on the forehead, he went into his own bedroom and closed the door behind him.

Light from the skylight above their bed reflected Dakota's gorgeous figure under the covers and he could tell that she was sound asleep. Still, after eight years of marriage, she was still just as gorgeous as she was the day he'd met her. Her body had filled out more after having two children and he loved every single curve.

He knew that she was having thoughts that he was stepping out on her, but that never, ever crossed his mind. He was dedicated to his wife even if he wasn't around as much as he should be. Women did make a point of flirting with him relentlessly and not once has he ever been tempted. To him, there was no other woman for him besides Dakota even if he failed to show her. She was drop-dead gorgeous and beautiful in every way, internally and externally. She was his everything.

Walking past the bed, he went straight to their bathroom and disrobed after turning on the shower. Moments after stepping inside, he could see Dakota's silhouette on the other side of the glass shower door. He opened it, hoping he could entice her to join him inside once she got a look at how her mere presence hardened every part of his body. There was never a time when he didn't want her. Making love to her was like breathing to him. She was a virgin when they'd met and he enjoyed her naiveté back then and then her aggressiveness when she learned what her body liked, wanted and needed. He smiled at her as she looked up and down his water and soap covered body.

"Like what you see?" he asked making sure to speak in a deep, sexy tone, laced with a hungriness to his voice and stare.

He watched as a stoic Dakota looked him up and down before her eyes finally landed on his face. He knew even the sight of him hard and ready for her wasn't having the impact he expected when her eyes didn't land on his manhood, a location that often got a lengthy stare from her. She didn't have the look that he was hoping for. He knew they'd had their struggles lately, but usually lovemaking was a good way for them to make-up and he needed that now. He didn't want any more animosity.

"The real question is, do you still like what you see?" she asked and when her words weren't accompanied by a smile, he knew they were coming from a place other than where he wanted her mood to be, which he hoped would be a sexy one. He had a feeling they were about to revisit the conversation from earlier in the night. He wasn't going there because his vision of the ending wasn't going to be with him buried deep inside of her.

"I always have and I always will love what I see, you know that," he replied as the water continued to cascade down his body, now wetting the bathroom floor with the shower door opened. He was disappointed when Dakota didn't make a move to join him, but instead moved to sit on one of the seats in front of the mirror, right across from the shower.

"Do I know that or do you just want me to always assume that? I wouldn't be able to tell from the lack of attention over the past several months. There was a time when you couldn't keep your hands off of me. You would come home in the middle of the day when you knew the kids would be napping and we'd have the best quickies that weren't really quickies. When the kids were with your sister, we would spend hours and hours in bed, on the floor, on the sofa, anywhere we wanted to be as long as I could feel you inside of me. Why do I feel like I'm the only one who notices a change in our love? You act as if things are as normal as they always have been, but they aren't. Are you seeing someone, Brandon? I noticed when I threw that out earlier in our phone conversation you ignored it."

Realizing a sexy lovemaking session was not about to take place in the shower, Brandon closed the shower door and finished quickly. Turning off the water, he stepped out and grabbed a towel from the rack to wrap around his waist.

"I ignored it because it's a ridiculous thought. Why the hell would you ask me something like that? I think there are some men who have wives who should ask that question, but you know me and I'm not one of those men. Is that who you think you're married to?" he asked, now beyond irritated.

"I asked because obviously I'd like to have an answer or I wouldn't have asked. Men are tempted every day and the distance between us lately gives me pause to wonder what the hell is going on and I don't want to hear work; there has to be more to it than that. So, are you?"

Grabbing another towel to dry off with, he walked over to her and looked down. He couldn't believe they were actually having a conversation about him cheating on her. Rather than fly off the handle, he responded calmly and looked at her directly.

"No, Dakota, I am not seeing anyone. I have

never cheated on you and I never will. There isn't another woman out here that I'd want. It's always been you and you know that."

"It used to be me, but I don't feel like that anymore," she said, solemnly.

"Baby, I opened the shower door hoping you would join me, but instead you want another fight and I'm tired. I don't feel like more of that tonight. If we're not going to make love and make up for all this fighting we've been doing lately, then fine, I'm going to bed. What I'm not going to do is stand in my bathroom and convince you that I'm not seeing anyone else. That's absurd and it's preposterous for you to even think that or to even ask me that."

Brandon turned away and walked back into the bedroom, followed close behind by a still pissed off Dakota. Neither turned on a light as he sat down on the side of the bed. Somehow things were taking a downward spiral and he couldn't figure out how they got here and hoped he had finally put an end to her insinuations.

3-Love on Top

Dakota walked into the bedroom, feeling better that he admitted to her that nothing outside of their marriage was going on, but something was and she couldn't let it go. She wanted back what was missing and if a middle of the night discussion is what it was going to take to get there, then she was ready for that.

"Baby, the one thing I've known about you from when we dated in college was your insatiable sexual appetite and it's always been like that, until lately. Back then I wondered if I could keep up or if I could continue to please you because I was lacking in knowledge of how to please a man. You taught me that and I've always been open to making sure that part of our marriage never lacked. I've tried sexy lingerie, I've tried planning getaways for us, I've called you in the middle of the day when the kids are out on play dates and you're always too busy even for midday rendezvous and now I'm out of ideas to keep your interest. What is it? What's wrong?" she begged.

Brandon could hear the hurt in her voice and he never wanted her to think that she wasn't enough for him. He would always want her, but business has been so hectic that he's had to retool his mind and focus on that. He didn't mean for his home life to suffer, but he hoped she'd be a little more patient with him.

"So, you think because our sex life isn't on fleek all day, every day that the answer is I'm cheating on you? I'm married to you – I love you and I know you know that," he explained.

"Have I become unattractive to you? Have I put on too much weight? Am I not what you want anymore? Tell me something because we're growing apart and I never expected that. I know you've been busy with business and that's taken a lot of your time, but you've always had time for me and the kids, but not so much lately.

Tonight, the kids were drawing family pictures and Braden drew one without you in it with us. Instead, he drew a picture of you working someplace off to the side. He should have been able to draw a picture of the four of us together. He's four years old and all he knows is his father works all the time. I put the kids in this camp for part of the day so that they could have more activities this summer with other kids and my plan was to take them out early so that we could end our summer taking a few trips. Now, you've backed out of that time with us and instead suggested I still take the trips with the kids and invite your sister. Alisha didn't move here to Miami to entertain me when you're busy. She moved here to manage one of your supper clubs, not turn into babysitter to take your place as if that would be okay. You're my husband and their father and we need you around."

Brandon exhaled loudly, not a fan of the direction the discussion was taking. He'd been up all day and all night and he was exhausted. He wanted to make love to her with the energy he did have left, but it seems as if that's the furthest thing from Dakota's mind.

"I am around and I plan on being around more, but Aiden and I have to strike while the iron is hot right now. There are a lot of new plans I haven't had a chance to tell you about because I know it would only make you angrier when all you'll be able to see is me being away even more. I'm trying my best to do all the right things here, but you complain about everything and after a long day of work, that's the last thing I need. I'll consider this round three after the fight yesterday in the morning and the one earlier on the phone and right now, I'm all talked out and I don't have any fight left in me. Baby, I love you and I want to get beyond this. I'm just asking for a little more patience."

Brandon stood and walked around to his side of the bed, dropped the towel and got in. He looked over at Dakota who was still standing on the other side of the bed. He waited to see if she was planning to continue the fight and when she didn't and instead climbed into bed, he hoped they could call a truce for the night. In a few short hours, the sun would be up and he had a construction meeting at eight in the morning, less than four hours away.

He didn't move while she found her comfortable place, which to his dismay, was as far away from him as she could get on their king-sized bed. Sliding all the way over to her and pressing his still naked body up to hers, he hoped he could again tempt her into putting their issues aside and coming together in more ways than one.

His body hardened the minute he made contact with hers. She was right about one thing and that was they hadn't had hot, passion sex in over a week and as tired as he was, he wasn't sure he'd be able to give it his all, but he wanted her and he wanted her to know that he wanted her, hoping she wanted him, too.

Pulling her snug up against his hardness, he rubbed his rock-hard flesh against the silk of her panties that barely covered her behind, a part of her that he loved to worship. She was a stunning woman and he couldn't understand how she could think he would ever find another woman who would satisfy him the way she did.

He smiled when Dakota looked over her shoulder at him. He didn't look at her face because he already knew the look that he would see there would say that he had some nerve after they'd just had a fight.

"Really, Brandon?" she asked, whispering then turning back the other way.

Brandon leaned forward and placed a kiss on the back of her neck. Reaching around in front, he grasped her breasts through the thin material of her loose-fitting tank top.

"Yes, really. Fight or no fight, what you feel is what you always do to me. I love you, Dakota. I miss you and I want you. How can you still be so mad? I'm here now and I want to make love to you and yet you're lying next to me like an ice princess. That's not like you. If nothing else, we have always been able to come together like this. You don't want me? You don't miss me?" he moaned in her ear.

Caressing her as her nipples pebbled between his fingers, he knew that she may be fighting him with her mind, but her body was coming over to the dark side and suddenly, he was feeling more energetic than ever.

"Yes, baby, I miss you, too and I love making love to you, but I need my Brandon back. I need the one who put his family first and not just at four in the morning."

Brandon was gaining even more energy when he felt her wiggle her behind back in his direction. He also knew he needed Dakota; he needed to feel her wrapped tightly around him and everything would be right in his world. For the time being, he wanted all thoughts of their fight out of their minds and he wanted them to focus only on feeling.

Placing open-mouthed kisses along her neck and shoulder, he felt the moment her body gave up the fight. Spooning her, he knew she could feel how hard he was and he knew there was no way he was going to be able to sleep in this state. Slipping his hand under her shirt, he fondled her breasts with vigor, the way he knew she loved and the moment he heard her moan, there wasn't a need for any more talking.

"That's it baby," he whispered in her ear before sucking the lobe in his mouth, feeling her squirm against him as he gyrated his hips in rhythm with hers.

"Yes," he heard her moan and knew she was losing the fight that was still in her over his absence.

He ground his hips into her backside causing his manhood to slip between her legs from behind. Sliding his hand down her body from her breasts, he slipped it inside the front of her panties until he encountered wetness and after his first stroke of the nub that had come out to greet him, more wetness covered his fingers.

"All this fighting is unnecessary. Believe me when I say that there's no other woman for me. No other woman could ever make me this hard. A mere thought of being with you does this to me and that has not changed since that first day at Norfolk State when I saw you and knew you would be mine. You are my one and only, Dakota – my one and only. Can you feel me, baby?" he said soft and seductively, adding little nips with his tongue and teeth along the column of her neck and across her shoulders. He smiled when he felt her open her legs slightly to give him better access to that warm place he loved so much.

With the extra room, Brandon slipped first one finger and then another inside of her and the minute she opened her mouth to sigh in ecstasy, he stroked faster in and out of her body, causing her hips to grind in sync with the movement of his fingers.

"I miss this," Dakota sighed as he held her tightly against him.

"I know and I'm sorry you've had to miss me like this. I've missed this too, feeling you come apart like this in my arms. It's pure exhilaration when I hear you moan and just when I think I can't possibly get any harder, I'm stiffening more, almost to the point of pain, but I need to feel you let go. Are you enjoying my fingers, baby?" he asked, breathlessly, barely able to hold on himself. He wanted inside of her badly, but first he needed this to be about her.

"Yes, Brandon. I can't hold on much longer," she

sighed through gritted teeth, trying not to scream and wake the kids.

When her body began to pump around his fingers stroking in and out of her body, he knew she was close and he wanted her over the top in pure ecstasy.

"Give it to me baby! You know what I want," he said and increased the tempo of his strokes even more. Even in the darkness, he could see her mouth form in that all too familiar "O" and knew she was there. He could feel her body rising and the moment her orgasm slammed into her and her hips bucked wildly on the bed, he combined more nips along her neck like she liked with his strokes in her body and added his thumb to caress her hardened nub. He continued his caresses as she rose higher and higher, turning her face into the pillow to smother her cries of pleasure. Without leaving any time for rest, Brandon slid her panties down her legs and the moment they were off, he positioned himself at her entrance and slid inside of her from behind. The moment he encountered the large amount of wetness at her entrance, he knew he wouldn't be able to last long himself. They loved various sexual positions and him behind her was one of their favorites.

Raising her leg and bending it a little for a better seated position inside of her, he began pumping into her slowly at first to the sound of her moans mixed with his own and letting the natural feeling to pleasure her take over, he increased the speed. He knew he was done for the minute Dakota threw her gorgeous ass back at him and after giving her an earth shattering orgasm, he felt her reaching for another and this time, he was with her. He pumped eagerly as she ground madly back into him.

As his world began to spin out of control with unadulterated lust, he felt the need to howl and knew what was in him would wake even the closest neighbor and their kids who slept in rooms across the hall from theirs, so he buried his head in the crook of Dakota's neck and groaned through his pleasure which seemed to last an eternity. His orgasm was so strong, he saw stars on the back of his eyelids which were tightly closed. It was this feeling that he'd been missing out on and he was happy to bring it back for them.

As their bodies calmed along with their breathing, Brandon moved to pull out of her body, knowing she had to feel uncomfortable with her leg in the air.

"No, don't," she said softly, still in a sexual haze.

"Baby, this can't be comfortable for you."

"I don't care about being comfortable. I don't want to break the connection. Stay inside of me," she pleaded.

Pulling her closer, he did as she asked, lowering her leg to a more comfortable position. Pulling the blanket up over them that had drifted down during their lovemaking, the only thing on his mind was how much he loved her and never wanted her to feel anything, but his love at all times, whether they were together or not. His love for her was everything and he was able to make it through each day because of her and the life they were building together.

"I love you, baby. I promise to do better. Don't give up on me or our love. Promise me you won't ever give up on me or think that your love isn't sufficient enough. It's more than enough and I promise I will figure something out. I know that I need to be around more for you and the kids."

"I love you, too and I'll always be right here for you. I'm sorry for getting out of control over this, but I was really missing you and I mean missing you like crazy here at home, in our lives and connected to my body like this. I'm here baby, I'm here."

Pulling Dakota as close to him as he possibly could, he drifted off, finally exhausted beyond being able to stay awake any longer. All he needed to hear was that she loved him; that's all he ever needed.

4~Love on Top

"Two days"! Dakota uttered.

"Two days of what?" Alisha asked.

"Your brother promised me. He promised me he would do better and that lasted two days. Three weeks later and we're back to where we were before."

Alisha followed Dakota through the ladies' department of a sexy lingerie store in Miami. While the kids were in camp, Dakota agreed to accompany her to the store to pick up a few things for her date with her boyfriend, Chris. She'd met Chris three months ago and they have been going hot and heavy ever since.

"Things still aren't any better, huh?" Alisha asked.

"No, and I think they've actually gotten worse. You know he flew to New York for some meeting the other day and he was supposed to be gone for two days and that turned into four because of some issue with the negotiation over the space they were trying to acquire. We made plans to take the kids to Disney World in Orlando which were cancelled and then I find he had this business trip he could suddenly find time to get away for. His consolation was to tell me we could still take the kids away and do something right after school started. I don't want to take a vacation after Jasmine has already started school. I need her to be focused on school, not distracted by vacation."

Alisha could not only hear, but see Dakota's frustration as she forcibly moved clothes around on the rack, not really looking at anything.

"So, he finally told you about the new game plan, huh? Aiden told me about it a while ago and he made me promise to not tell you because Brandon wanted to have a discussion with you, knowing you wouldn't be happy about it."

"I don't want you or him to think I'm not happy for all of the success they've achieved. What they've done is amazing and when Forbes magazine did that article on them and their business acumen, I couldn't have been prouder. Sometimes I feel like a selfish bitch for wanting more of him, but shouldn't I want that?" Dakota asked as she looked through the racks of sexy underwear.

"Ooh, that is sexy!" Alisha exclaimed at a naughty pair of thong, laced panties and demi-cup matching bra in bright red.

"Brandon loves me in red underwear or should I say he used to love me in red underwear. Now, we're like passing strangers in the night. He comes in after the kids and I are asleep and is gone before we get up in the morning. I don't even think he'd notice if I wore this at night."

Dakota held it up to get an even better look at it and could imagine it on and Brandon ripping it off of her. He'd be so inflamed with want for that area between her legs that he wouldn't be able to resist his carnal desire for her. There were times when he could be like a wild animal in his lovemaking and she loved it. Those were the days, she thought silently.

"Girl, trust me he'd notice."

Dakota put it back on the rack and looked around.

"Well, we're not here to shop for me, we're her to shop for you and your night of degradation I'm not sure I even want to know about."

Alisha laughed.

"Yes, and it will be down and dirty. Chris isn't like any other guy I've gone out with and the fact that he isn't African American hasn't bothered me at all. I've been getting a second glance from some of my friends when I introduce him, but that's because they have issues, not me. My man is hot and he treats me like a queen."

"Is this the first time you've dated outside your

race?" Dakota asked.

She was surprised when Alisha first introduced Chris to her and her brothers. No one cared what race he was, but her brothers did make it clear to him that he'd better treat their sister like a princess and according to Alisha, he had been doing that from the minute they met and as happy as she knew Alisha was, she couldn't be anything, but happy for her.

"It is and you know how much I've always loved the brothers, but there is no need to walk through life looking at race. For me, it's about the connection and he and I connected from the start just like you and Brandon did during our days back at Norfolk State."

"What is this big celebration you're having?" Dakota asked.

"Oh, I forgot to tell you that part when I invited you to come shopping with me. Chris just passed the bar and got a job with a big law firm here in Miami. I'm going to cook him an amazing meal before he leaves for Chicago to visit his family."

"Have you met them yet?"

Alisha could tell by the look on Dakota's face that her hesitation in responding didn't go unnoticed.

"No, not yet. His family isn't as forward thinking as we are and he doesn't want to subject me to them yet. He doesn't have the best relationship with his father who has been known for a bit of bigotry over the years. He's visiting them to let them know that he's in love with me and he expects them to support our love like they have supported everything else he's ever done. He originally wanted me to go, but with Brandon out of town, Aiden needs me to oversee both supper clubs. We're planning to visit them sometime in the next several months for some party they're having for his sister's wedding announcement. Did I tell you that his sister is marrying a guy she doesn't love, but it's someone their father picked out for her because of friendship and partnership. According to Chris, it's messy, but he's the son of some rich guy involved in shipping or something, business his father is trying to get a foot in the door with. I don't know if I'm ready to be exposed to that foolishness, but I'm readier than Chris is. I told him we can't avoid his family forever."

"Are you excited about this new love of yours?" Dakota asked.

"I am. I'm excited about where my relationship with him is and where it's going. I've never been this happy before. Now, what do you think about this?"

Alisha held up a very skimpy white and black thong and bra set that had ties at the hip of the panties and a tie in the front of the bra, making it easy to get both off of her."

"Oh, I love that. You should definitely get that one. You should also get the little silver one-piece naughty nightie you picked up when we first arrived."

"Okay, I'll do that as long as you agree to get the red set I saw you put back and find a few other items, too. Don't you dare give up on my brother because he's being a bone head and thinking only about work. I told Aiden he's the single one in the mix and he should take up more of the slack, so that Brandon can have time to focus more on you guys. I've been pushing them for weeks to hire more help and that's something I know they've been planning to do. They shouldn't have to work this hard now that they have blown up. They need to hire competent people to run things and find more time to enjoy the rewards of all of their hard work."

"I've been saying that to Brandon, but it's like talking to a brick wall. I think things are only going to get worse once the new club is up and running. How is that going? Brandon doesn't tell me much and I'm sure it's because I harbor so many ill feelings about the state of our marriage that he doesn't think I'll be interested in what's going on."

Dakota knew she needed to do better in that area. She never wanted Brandon to feel like he couldn't share his successes with her.

"It's going great. The new club will have an office park built next to it and we're moving the offices for the company from the smaller building into this new space. I'm going to have an office in there and I can't wait to decorate it. The current office staff of fifteen should be at least thirty by now, but I know that expansion takes time and they're focused on the construction and not what it takes to run the company. I think things will turn around soon. I want you to have faith that my brother loves you and he'll get it right soon."

Dakota didn't respond as thoughts entered her mind again that there is a possibility that Brandon could be seeing someone else. Though he told her that was as far from the truth as she could get, she was again questioning it because of the distance between them.

"Alisha, I want to ask you something and I know we're only friends and Brandon is your brother, but I hope you would answer me honestly if you know."

Hearing the seriousness in her voice, Alisha turned to face her full on.

"What's going on? We're more than just friends, so don't go there with that we're just friends thing. We're closer than most sisters are, now lay it on me."

"Don't think I'm crazy or discount my feelings easily with what I'm about to say, okay?"

"Spill it, Dakota."

"Okay, I think Brandon is seeing someone else. If he were and you knew about it, would you tell me?" she asked, unsure if they should even be having this conversation.

When Alisha didn't immediately respond, she thought the worst-case scenario. Maybe Brandon was cheating on her.

"Dakota! I'm trying my best not to call you crazy, but you are out of your mind! Brandon would never, ever do anything like that. Now, Aiden is the playboy and I wouldn't trust him to be faithful to any woman, but that's not Brandon. From day one, he's been about you and only you."

Dakota exhaled knowing she was being foolish, but something had to give.

"I asked him and he gave me an unequivocal no, but I don't know what's wrong. I'm not sure he finds me attractive anymore or at least not like he had before I popped out two children and gained a little weight."

Alisha looked at her from her head to her feet.

"Weight? What weight? Girl, there isn't a woman around who wouldn't want to gain the weight in the places that you have, post-babies. You and I work out all the time and I know you're in good shape. You filled out in all of the places a man loves and my brother is no exception. I've seen how he looks at you and I always feel like I'm in the middle of the start of an X-rated movie when I'm around the two of you. I get the feeling that I should exit a room quietly before he jumps your bones right in front of me, impatiently," she laughed.

For the first time in days, Dakota laughed out loud at the image.

"I can always depend on you to make me feel better. I just can't shake the late nights and the phone ringing at all hours of the night and him shutting it off. I see how women flirt with him and they know he's married. You know women these days don't care anything about a ring on a man's finger. Those are usually the men they go after first and Brandon is fine and rich. Many people say he has a familiar look to the guy who plays Ghost on that HBO show called, "Power". He's just as sexy as that guy. What's his name?" she asked.

"You mean Omarion Hardwick? That brother is insanely gorgeous. My brother does favor him a lot and women often ask if he's related to him. They try to use it as a ploy to draw him in to see if he'd bite, but he never does because all he knows is his wife. Trust me, all this time Brandon is messing up, it's all about business and not about a chick or chicks on the side. If for any reason I thought otherwise, I would not only tell you, but I'd help you hide the body, girl! You know I don't play that kind of mess from any man and definitely not from my brother. Aiden can do his thing because he's still single, but if he were married, they know I wouldn't stand behind anything foolish like cheating. I told you how they were with Chris when I told them how serious the relationship was. They practically had him jacked up against the outside of the house making sure he understood that if he mistreated me, they would be all over him without mercy. Chris and I laughed it off, but he also told me that he understood where they were coming from. They are out to protect me and expect that any man I date would treat me with the utmost respect."

Dakota shook her head remembering that same discussion with Brandon who relayed to her what happened that night.

"I remember Brandon telling me about that encounter. I couldn't believe they did that. He tried to blame it all on Aiden saying he simply went along with it, but I have a feeling Brandon was the ringleader."

"True and that's why I know he wouldn't do that to you. Trust me, it's not about another woman. It's about business and Brandon needs to take a fresh look at what is being sacrificed and do the right thing. I believe he will, just don't give up on him."

"I would never give up on him. Not in a million years would I do that. I just want my husband back and I want us to have a life that's about more than making more money. Most people would love to have seven figures in the bank. We do and it seems it's still not enough for him. I would be lying if I said I didn't love the fact that financially we are secure, but I want security in our love and I feel like it's slipping away."

Alisha looked through the racks and pulled out the red set she saw Dakota eyeing.

"I bet if he saw you in this, he wouldn't be slipping and sliding in the opposite direction of you. Get it and you'll know when the right time will be to lay this on him. He won't know what hit him.

Now, let's see what else we can get our hands on because after this, I want to take a trip to the sex toy shop. I don't want to hear another word about you doubting the love the two of you share. I look at you and all I can think about is relationship goals. I know there are some struggles, but when I look at the full scope of your love, it's admirable and I'd take it in a flash. I know how hot you two are for each other all the time. Remember, I shared a room with you back in college and though our scarf agreement on the door when we had company was in full effect when Brandon was in town, you forgot that the walls were not sound proof. I hope my niece and nephew are spared all that huffing and puffing!"

Alisha chuckled and then turned back to the racks, while cutting an eye at Dakota who could barely contain her surprise.

Dakota gasped and then laughed.

"I know you're not talking. I do recall things getting pretty hot and heavy with you and that quarterback."

"That was nothing compared to you and my brother and it was my brother. Ugh, you two were disgusting."

"Whatever. Why are we going to a sex toy shop?"

"Like you've never shopped there before," Alisha countered.

"I....I," was all Dakota could get out because she knew she couldn't lie her way out.

"Oh, don't try and get all innocent acting with me. I grew up with two hormones for brothers and I know they are off the chain when it comes to this kind of stuff. Besides, those stores have the best oils for massages and I love any reason to get my hands all over Chris's body."

Dakota laughed again, took the red outfit from Alisha's hand and picked up two others that she'd had her eyes on. She and Brandon had fallen back into a routine of arguing and fighting lately, but that didn't mean that she was losing hope that they would find their way back to each other. She felt better hearing Alisha say that she didn't believe Brandon was cheating on her. She didn't want to believe it. She just didn't know what else to think or do. Her husband was sexy as hell and everywhere they went, women made eyes at him, a lot of time totally disrespecting her, but Brandon has never disrespected her and she felt ashamed that she ever thought that he would.

"I think I would like to take a trip to that store. I want some of those handcuffs with the fur on them. If I ever get the chance to slow Brandon down, I want to be sure he doesn't get away until I want him, too."

"Yes!" Alisha shouted.

Dakota looked around and laughed, too, as other patrons in the store stared at them.

"You are going to get us thrown out of here. Let's get moving. I want to grab lunch and get home to get a few things done before I have to pick the kids up."

"Plus, you'll need time to hide all the naughty things I know you're going to find at our next stop."

Dakota didn't comment, but she was planning on getting a few extras for Brandon and for her.

5-Love on Top

Dakota was at the gym working out and was happy for the time to herself. She was expecting Brandon home later in the day. This was Brandon's second trip out of town in two weeks and while the kids were at camp for their last week, she was happy to have time to still keep in shape. She may have gained some weight after having two kids, but her body was still toned. Her stomach was flat and there was no flab or fat to speak up. Her behind was high and toned and though she's always had large breasts, something she knew Brandon loved about her from when they first met, hers were still round and firm and thanks to great exercise and weight training, they didn't sag.

She grew up self-conscious about her large breasts, but as she got older, she loved her shape more and more. With the rest of her body filling out, she should never feel like she was lacking in a way that she couldn't keep her husband interested.

The gym was the place where she not only worked out, but she found time to swim, spend time in the steam bath and crystal salt room, one of her favorites. This is where she could get away from the cares of the world and just enjoy time indulging in herself. Today, she was planning to take advantage of the massage room and also get a manicure and pedicure.

She and Brandon had at one time, planned to work out together and work on helping each other stay in shape, but his schedule was so crazy that she found they were going at two different times and never on the same days. He preferred going late at night and she preferred the middle of the day.

Her mind was on him since she knew he was returning from his latest business trip to New York where he ended up being for five days. She missed him and though they talked every day, several times a day, it wasn't the same. The kids loved hearing him talk about New York and he sent them pictures of everything he was seeing and he promised that he would take them there one day very soon. She hoped that wasn't another promise he was making that he'd have to end up breaking as he'd been doing with other promises lately.

Taking a break before her scheduled massage time, she grabbed her water bottle and sat at one of the tables and watched others work out. She was suddenly startled by the presence of someone standing on the side of her. She looked up into the face of one of the men she saw working out at the gym often. He was older and a sign that men of any age could maintain well, solid physiques.

"Hey there!" he said cheerfully.

"Hello," she replied.

"I hope I'm not interrupting you."

"No, not at all."

"Great. Do you mind if I sit? I'm waiting on my wife to finish her workout and I know I've seen you around here a few times. Your table has the only open chairs and I don't want to intrude."

"Oh, no not at all. Feel free to have a seat. I think I've seen you and your wife in here on several occasions," she said.

"Yes, she loves this place. We try to carve some time out at least once a week to work out together. Are you and your husband working out also?" he asked. Dakota noticed he was looking at her large wedding ring.

"No, just me. He's crazy busy with work and he likes to work out in the evenings."

"Cool. It's a great facility. By the way, I'm Jason and my wife over there is Artis."

He held out his hand and Dakota shook it.

"I'm Dakota."

"Nice to meet you, Dakota. Have you checked out any of the other amenities besides the gym?"

"I have and today I'm going to try a massage, but

my favorite is the hot tub and the steam room. The heat of both allow me to de-stress my mind."

"You should ask my wife about the Pilates class. She loves that and it's the first thing she does when we come here. She's making her way over here now."

Dakota looked up as the woman came over to their table.

"Hello," she said and Dakota shook her extended hand.

"Babe, this is Dakota. She was gracious enough to let me share her table until you were finished. You look like you could use some water. Your bottle was empty when I picked it up. Sit here in my seat and I'll go get you a bottle."

Jason stood and walked toward the main counter.

"Thanks. I'm Artis. I hope my husband didn't bore you with too much chatter. He loves talking to people. As a college professor, you would think he would like a break from talking to people whenever he could get one, but not him. Is your husband here with you?" Artis asked and looked around like she was expecting a man to walk up.

"No, he's working. He comes in the evening. I get to come when our kids are at camp during the day."

"Great idea. Our kids are pretty much adults with our last, at eighteen, getting ready to go away to college and we finally get our lives back."

"That must be nice to finally have that time

together after raising kids. Mine are seven and four and we still have a long way to go."

"It wasn't easy, but we have always looked forward to this time. Now is when the real fun begins."

"You know, your husband mentioned something about Pilates class. I've never done that. Can you tell me about it? Do you like it?"

"Oh, I love it," Artis said and enthusiastically began sharing about her experience.

Dakota sat back and listened.

~~

After rushing home from the airport, Brandon knew he had a little time before he'd have to make his way to the club later in the evening and he was hoping to catch Dakota at the gym. They always talked about working out together and with him being gone for most of the past two weeks, this last time for five days and with the kids at camp, he was hoping they could have some time to work out, maybe do lunch and then talk.

They were back to arguing all the time and after that night where they'd made love a few weeks back after the fight in the bathroom, he was hoping they'd be back on track. Of course, they'd made love several times since then, but he didn't like how it felt rushed because he was always on his way to his next stop, fitting her in between. He knew that something had to give or he'd lose his wife. He could feel her attention slipping away.

Walking into the gym, he looked around for her. He saw her white BMW in the parking lot and knew she was still there. He'd seen the note she left for him on the refrigerator at home, knowing he would probably get in before she returned. Stopping at the counter, he looked around and saw her talking to a man and watched as the guy stood and walked in his direction as a woman sat in his place. He started to walk over to the table, but the man struck up a conversation with another guy as he was waiting to pay for a bottle of water. His ears perked up when he heard the man say his wife's name.

"Who's the woman your wife is talking to?" the other guy asked.

The guy who had been sitting at the table looked back at the table and smiled.

"Oh, her name is Dakota. This place is so crowded, she had the only extra chair in the place and that made me a lucky son of a bitch, I tell ya. I've seen her in here a few times and I have to say she is an incredibly beautiful woman."

"Is she married? I know you are, so pull it back," the guy laughed.

"I may be married, but I'm not dead and I know a lonely woman when I see one and that one my brother, is a lonely woman. She's married, but I've never seen her in here with her husband. I did ask her and she said he likes to work out at night due to work or something. Whatever his excuse is, he's a fool. I would spend all of my time with a beautiful woman like that and work or no work, I'd make the time."

"Don't tell me you were flirting with her?"

"I wish. I don't get the vibe that she would be receptive to flirting or anything else, but you never know. Leave a woman alone enough, especially one who isn't getting the attention she wants, she may be open to just about anything from a man who will give it to her. You know I love Artis, but Dakota makes my body jump every time I see her. I would buy that woman an island if I could get her to go out on a date with me."

"Did you just say she was married? She's not going out on a date with you?"

"Hey, I didn't say she was and I didn't ask her. I'm just saying, every time I see here, she's either with another young woman around her age or she's alone. Like I said, I've been married long enough to know a lonely woman when I see one."

"What happened to that woman you were seeing?"

"Veronica? She started breaking my pockets and making demands on my time. I told her from the start I wasn't leaving Artis, but she wanted more and more. She was even talking about leaving her husband. I told you, all it takes is showing these lonely women the attention their husbands don't show them and they soon begin to do things they never thought they would do."

"Looks like her and Artis are having a good

chat."

"Yeah, I see that. Maybe they'll become friends and I'll get an eyeful of Dakota on a more consistent basis."

"She is beautiful and look at that killer body. I see the men ogling her when she's here and she has never flirted with anyone, though she could have her pick."

"Yeah, she's probably lonely, but not desperate for attention yet, but if that husband isn't on his game, it's only a matter of time. When will men learn to make their wives a priority. I may have stepped out on Artis a few times, but I know for a fact that I give her the time and attention she needs to be sure she's never one of these lonely married women I see walking around. As a man who has stepped out a time or two, I still have advice for every married man with a fine ass wife like her and that is, pay more attention to your woman before some other man does."

"I hear you. I'll catch you at the gym next week?"

"We'll be here."

With that, Brandon was fuming to the point that he wanted to knock the guy out for targeting his wife. If he were honest, he couldn't be mad if another man noticed how lonely his wife was. He was a damn fool and he knew it. Dakota had been begging him for more time and attention and he'd been too focused on work to see that he was slipping in the husband department. He knew that women could be coerced into side relationships with other men even if they start out innocent, all because some man wasn't paying enough attention to his wife, like he wasn't. He watched as Dakota laughed with the couple and she appeared to be having a good time.

He was no longer in the mood to work out, so he turned around and went back out of the gym, headed to his car and headed home. How had his life gotten here? He knew he'd had big dreams when he and Dakota first got married and once the businesses began taking off, he wanted bigger and better and worked towards that, while at the same time, his marriage, his love was suffering. He wasn't doing a good job balancing both and he had no one to blame, but himself.

6~Love on Top

Dakota opened the garage door and was surprised to see Brandon's car in his spot. He must be home because his truck was in the garage's third spot and his motorcycle was also there. She expected him to return and head straight for the club after stopping at the house to drop off his luggage and seeing that no one else was home.

"Looks like Daddy's home," she said to the kids, who quickly jumped out and ran into the house with cheers of daddy, daddy.

Grabbing their bags from the backseat, she reminded herself to tell Jasmine to stop letting Braden out of his car seat. She didn't want him getting used to that and jumping out when they were other places, risking getting hit by a car. She would tackle that discussion later, knowing the excitement the kids were experiencing with

Brandon being home and it was still daylight.

Walking into the house, she encountered them talking a mile a minute sharing their day with him. It was rare for them to see him home this time of day, so she didn't want to interrupt and let them have their time.

"I'm just coming from the gym, so I'm going to grab a shower and change my clothes. Welcome home," she said.

She felt odd because she knew that she should have given Brandon, who had been gone for five days, a better welcome home greeting that included a kiss, but all she wanted to do was get a shower. Deep down, she was still angry that he'd been gone away on business again and for each of those days while he was gone, they argued on the phone more than they shared love over the phone.

Dakota headed for the stairs and went straight to the bathroom for her shower. She hadn't been in there too long and after washing her hair to get the salt out from the crystal salt room at the gym, she exited the shower to find Brandon unpacking his suit case on the bed. She didn't say anything as she walked to her closet and put on underclothes, shorts and a t-shirt. She turned around to see him standing in the doorway.

"How was the trip?" she said, breaking the ice. There was still so much tension between them.

"It was fruitful. We got the space and all the paperwork was signed."

"Well, that's exciting. I'm happy for you," she said, walking around him to go back into the bedroom.

"Are you? I can't tell. You're really keeping your excitement contained," he retorted.

"Trying to be a smartass?" she asked facetiously.

"Not really trying to be, but I'm wondering what's wrong with you. I've been gone for five days and I come home and the first thing you want to do is get out of my presence."

"Where are the kids?" she asked, walking around the room and taking his dirty clothes from the suit case to add to the laundry basket she already had sitting on the floor.

"I gave them a snack and turned on the Disney channel. They're fine, but I think you and I aren't. I've apologized a million times about this trip, but it couldn't be helped. I know it came right on the heels of the last trip, but that couldn't be avoided. I couldn't leave in the middle of negotiations."

"I have no doubt you couldn't because that's how much dedication you put into something that's important to you, unlike, oh, I don't know, unlike me or the kids."

Her derision at the moment was crystal clear.

"That's not fair, Dakota."

"No, it's not fair, but it's the truth."

Brandon walked over to her.

"Baby, I'm trying here. I came home today and I'm here now."

Dakota stopped sorting his clothes and turned around to face him.

"Oh yeah? Are you home for the rest of the evening after being gone for five days? Are we going to make plans tonight for a family trip or is that cancelled again?" She held up her hand to stop him when she saw him about to offer another excuse. "No need to answer. I'm sure you have to go check on the club tonight and I'll do what I always do and entertain our kids, give them dinner and put them to bed before putting myself to bed. It's a good thing I stopped by the sex toy shop and bought myself a companion. Who knows when I'll get the attention from a living, breathing human man in the form of my husband again."

Being sarcastic was becoming her norm, but it was all she had to offer at the moment.

Brandon started to come back at her in anger, but he didn't. He could see she was hurting and his mind went back to the conversation he'd overheard at the gym between the two guys. She was giving him clue after clue that she was lonely. She was right that he had to go to the club. Aiden had been running everything since he'd been gone and he wanted to give him a break; he owed him that much.

"I'm not even going to comment on your little quip about a sex toy because you're being mean. I get it, I'm not giving you enough attention."

"Yet, you promised me you were going to do

better. For two days after that conversation and you got your four in the morning orgasm, you came home and spent time with me and the kids while we were still awake and then it was back to business as usual and then I find you have locked yourself into new deals that will now take you out of town on business. How the hell do you expect me to feel? All I want is my husband and all he wants is to make his next million-dollar business deal."

Dakota turned away from him and went back to the clothes.

"Where would we be without me making these deals? We wouldn't have this house, our cars, our daughter going to that expensive private school, all that money in the bank, you being able to do whatever you want and not have to check your bank balance. I'm doing what I'm doing for you and the kids and you should know that. This is all for us."

"When do we get to the us, Brandon? When is enough money enough for you to at least take a few weeks off for a vacation with your wife and kids? Our Disney trip, down the drain. Our plans for the beach, down the drain. Our plans to take them to amusement parks now that Braden is old enough to enjoy them, down the drain. We have the money to do lots of things, yet we don't do anything, but argue like we're doing right now and I'm tired of it. I don't want to fight and I don't want to discuss this anymore. I don't want to hold you up from the next place you need to be. I have laundry to do and since our plans for this weekend with the kids have been cancelled, I'm going to try to find some local activities for them to do. Don't let us get in the way of your next big business deal."

Dakota didn't give Brandon a chance to come back with a response. She grabbed the clothes basket, stormed out of their bedroom and slammed the door on her way out. She was breathing hard by the time she took the steps downstairs, checked on the kids and headed to the laundry room off the kitchen. Her heavy breathing was the only thing that kept her from balling out crying. She shouldn't have to feel this lonely in a loving marriage; she shouldn't, she thought and took her focus off of her troubles and started a load of laundry. A few minutes later, she heard the garage door open and close and knew that Brandon had left. They weren't getting anywhere and she was so angry that fixing their problems was the last thing on her mind.

"Mommy, I'm hungry," Braden said from the other room.

"I'm coming and just like that, she had to refocus from drama and on to a happier place like the needs of her children.

Her cell phone rang the moment she walked into the kitchen.

"Hey, Alisha!" she exclaimed, happy for the distraction while she started dinner.

"Hey. What are you doing over the weekend? Chris is heading to Chicago to visit his family and I have a free weekend. I'm off from the supper club until Tuesday and we could get into something if you want even if you want to get a babysitter or we can do something during the day with the kids."

"I think I'm going to find some local activities for the kids to do since Brandon again cancelled plans for a family outing."

"How was his trip to New York?" Alisha asked.

Dakota gasped in frustration knowing the last thing she wanted to do was rehash anything that had to do with Brandon and New York, but there was no need to take her frustration out on her sister-in-law.

"He said it was fine, but we didn't get too into it because we ended up fighting and he left to go to the club."

"Oh, things are still bad, huh? I'm heading over to the club in a few to talk to them about new staff I need to hire for the supper clubs. I'm doing interviews all next week and I want to make sure they're good with the number of people I'm looking to fill positions at both locations."

"Things are really bad between us. We can't get past a few words before it turns into an argument and I'm out of options now."

"Did you try the new lingerie yet?" Alisha asked.

"On who? On the new toy I bought? I get more mileage out of that these days than I get out of Brandon. I'm sick of his three in the morning booty calls. I want him to invest time in us, not give me what's left over from his day."

"I hear you and I'm sorry things have gotten worse. Are you sure you don't want to do anything this weekend? Maybe I can hang with you and the kids? That would be fun, right?"

"That would be great. You know my kids love you more than they love me. I swear I think even they believe I had them for you. Let me think of some things to do and we'll catch up tomorrow. It's the kids' last day at camp and they have the closing exercise. There is a big festival on Saturday with games and rides and I think they'll love that. I'm going to take them to the beach on Sunday for the day. We live right here in Miami and never go to the beach," she quipped.

"That's because we know better. We know to let the tourist have the beach and we swim in our own pools. Don't you know that's one of the reasons I love being at your house? It's all about that in-ground pool you have!" Alisha laughed out loud.

"Right! I'm going to finish cleaning up and get the kids in bed early for their last day tomorrow. It will be a busy one with closing activities. I reminded Brandon, but he told me he has some investor coming in and he won't be able to make it. I promised to take lots of pictures which I will, but not share with him. He should be there in person. I'm in a very petty mood today," she said trying to have a reason to smile.

"Don't be too mad at him. I don't want to pick

sides because you know I'd side with the kids on this one," Alisha said adding more humor to lighten the conversation.

"I know, I know. Are you planning on coming to their program tomorrow?"

"Of course. My brother may be stupid right now, but I'm not. There is no way I'd miss it. I'll see you tomorrow."

"At least one of you Kings has some sense," Dakota said and hung up.

"Mommy, come see what I made!" Jasmine shouted.

"Okay, I'll be right in."

Putting on her happy mommy face, she smiled with excitement and joined them at the table in the family room.

7-Love on Top

Brandon walked into the club without taking notice of the men he walked by that greeted him. He didn't see the looks of bewilderment on their faces as he passed by without giving one acknowledgment. His mood was on nine hundred and the last thing he wanted to do was hold a conversation about anything. He knew the moment he pulled into the parking lot that he should turn around and cool off after his blowout with Dakota, but he thought diving into work would take his mind off of the constant bickering the two of them seemed to get into every day. Their latest fight was their worst and he couldn't seem to shake the uneasiness he felt about the state of his marriage.

Taking the stairs to the third level instead of the elevator, he walked into his office and slammed the door behind him, falling into his office chair with such force, it startled him with thoughts of it collapsing to the floor under his weight.

"Pull it together," he said to himself.

"Yeah, you need to do that."

Brandon looked up at the sound of his brother's voice as he entered the office and closed the door behind him. He hadn't taken notice of who was standing in the bar area when he walked by, but should have known his brother would be among them. It was close to the time to get the club open where a line of guests had already formed outside of the front entrance and they were still an hour away from opening. He and Aiden both spent every waking hour at the club while construction was taking place at the new site. As much as he loved chats with his brother, now was not the time.

"Not now, Aiden," he said, turning around in his chair and looking out over the entire club floor. From his office, he could see everything happening in the club, yet no one could see up and into his office, giving him the privacy he loved and really needed at the moment.

He heard Aiden walk over and sit down across from him in the large brown leather sofa that stretched along the wall opposite him. He loved that chair and caught winks on it when he could after spending hour after hour at the club day in and day out. He wasn't in the mood to talk, but it was clear Aiden didn't care.

"I'd say now is as good a time as any other. What

gives? You walked by us like a growling grizzly as if we weren't standing there. We've had to deal with your moods a lot lately and being your brother, I took it upon myself to let you know how much of an ass you've been lately. You want to tell me what's going on or do you plan on continuing the war path, making everyone uncomfortable? Is this still about Dakota? Are you two still fighting?"

Exhaling his frustration, Brandon knew no one could read him like Aiden. They were not only fraternal twin brothers, only a few seconds apart, they were best friends. If there was anyone he could lay everything going on in his life out to, it was Aiden.

"Yes, it's still Dakota. I don't know what she wants, man. I give her everything and I work this hard to make sure her and the kids will never, ever want for anything and she still complains about every little thing. She knows how much work is involved with opening up the second night club and now that she knows about the club in New York and the one in California, our fighting is on a level I've never seen before. Not one sentence is shared between us without it turning into a full-blown bout. I don't know if we can make it back from all this fighting. Tonight, I actually walked out without even saying goodbye because she pissed me off. She acts like I'm never at home."

"Really dude? This is me you're talking to. You're never at home and neither am I, but the difference is, I don't have a wife and children at home who need me just as must as my business does."

Brandon finally turned around in his chair and faced Aiden.

"What am I supposed to do? Should I not take opportunities when they drop in our laps? Being this successful takes time and I'm doing this for them."

"No, you're doing this for you, don't get it twisted."

"Okay, then tell me where you see a compromise. We are working around the clock on these deals and they have to be done."

"If you're really willing to listen, I can answer that, but not if you're going to pacify me and only act like you're listening."

"Hit me with it," Brandon said.

Aiden leaned forward in his chair and placed his hands on his knees.

"For starters, you don't have to do everything the way you have been. Sometimes, I get the feeling you don't even trust me to handle certain things. We spend our days in the office or at the construction site and our nights either at the club or the restaurants. We have been saying for months that we need to hire more people to run things and not just waiter or cooking staff. I'm talking about hiring executive positions at the office to run things so that we don't have to be there every day. I could have gone to New York for at least one of the meetings or even both, but you decided without discussing it with me that you would take both meetings and you wanted me here to oversee operations in Miami while you were gone. We talked about making Alisha an equal partner in the supper clubs because she's been doing a great job running them and that way she can handle the day to day and hire the team she needs to manage, giving her a break sometimes. Bro, we are doing it all because we choose to, not because we have to. You are doing more than you really have to and in return what you're getting is a messed-up home life and there is no one to blame, but you. Let's do some of the things we said we were going to do as far as hiring more people that I'd like to have in place before the office park and the new club are finished. There is no way we can continue to operate at this level. We are going to burn each other out."

"Wow, tell me how you really feel," Brandon said and laughed, knowing that everything Aiden said was true and he was the cause of his problems and no one else.

"I'm being honest and that's what you've always gotten from me. The question is what are you going to do about it?"

"I have to do something because there is no way I'm losing my wife because of business. No way in hell is that ever going to happen. I have to get back in her good graces and once and for all, show her and not just tell her that my love for her tops everything else going on in my life."

"You and Dakota have the kind of love that I have always admired. You are one lucky bastard and I've said that a time or two in the past. I know your desire to be bigger and better in the business world because I've been on this path with you, but you have to admit, you are away from home a lot and I think it's time you focused more on Dakota, Jasmine and Braden than you are on business. I don't want you to think things will crumble if you aren't involved all day, every day. We have been in business for ten years, have made millions and are about to make more and if you are letting your personal life suffer because of it, all this work will mean nothing if you look back and find that you have lost the best thing that has ever happened to you. You know there was only a handshake between you meeting Dakota first and me meeting her first, right? I could have your life, man!" Aiden quipped.

"You may be thirty-eight seconds older than me, but I will pick you up and toss you from this third floor," Brandon joked.

Aiden threw his hands up in surrender.

"Hey, I'm just stating the obvious."

"You forgot to leave out the fact that our sister specifically introduced her to me and not you because she knew how much of a dog you were back then and pretty much still are and she knew Dakota deserved someone like me who would love and cherish her and only her."

"From your mouth to God's ears. If that's how you feel then do that. If she says you have been slacking, pick up your game and do what you need to do."

"I hear you and I know. I've been taking her punches like a champ because I know she's right, but there's a lot to do."

"There is and we have enough money to make things happen for us whether we are present twenty-four-seven or not. Let's make it happen and help you get your wife back."

"Let's make what happen?"

Aiden and Brandon looked up as Alisha entered the office.

"Hey, sis!" Brandon said.

"Hey, what's going on?" she asked.

"Well, Aiden here was telling me that I've been a jerk who has been ignoring my husband and fatherly duties at home when I don't have to. We were also talking about the new team of employees we need to hire at the office before the office park is completed and we move in as well as here at the club. I've been tossing around the idea of hiring two general managers to run this place and three for the new club."

"That's a great idea. I've been trying to get you to move in that direction for a while now," Alisha added.

Aiden joined the conversation.

"We're also tossing around the idea of making

you an equal partner in the supper clubs, splitting everything evenly between the three of us and letting you take over the everyday task of running them."

Alisha looked from one brother to the other, shocked to hear they wanted to have her as a partner. The thought never crossed her mind.

"Are you serious?" she asked.

"We are. We appreciate you uprooting your life and moving here to Miami to help us out and the supper clubs are doing better than ever right now and you have taken over most of the responsibility anyway. We thought now would be a good time to let them loose in your hands. What do you say?" Brandon asked.

Alisha responded with no hesitation. She was coming into the club tonight to talk to them about new staff and she walked into a partnership.

"I say yes and I appreciate the confidence you have in me."

"Hey, when you have a sister with a master's degree in marketing and business management, you use that to your advantage. We don't need to get into the details about this now, but we'll need to have a sit down about it soon to iron everything out."

"Not any time soon though because Brandon here is about to take some much-needed time and fix his home life and I don't want to see him around here until he does," Aiden said, standing to prepare to leave out.

Alisha looked at Brandon when she thought she saw signs of him about to object.

"If you're about to counter, don't try it. I've been talking to Dakota and it saddens me to hear that she is questioning her looks and her ability to still attract you because you've been too busy to take the time and pay more attention to your wife. If a man had done that to me, you and Aiden would be all over him."

"You know, I wasn't going to counter. I was going to say I need your help with an idea," he said as one idea after another entered his mind.

"If it means you and Dakota will be back on track, I will do whatever you need me to do," Alisha admitted.

"So, will I," Aiden added.

"Aiden, all I need from you is to look after everything for two weeks. I'm going to spend some time with my wife first and then time with her and the kids, which is where you come in Alisha. If you're not busy this weekend, I need you to look after the kids at least until Tuesday. I know you're off from the supper club anyway," he said, hoping that was still her plan.

"I am off and I was scheduled to hang with Dakota and the kids this weekend, but I can definitely make the time and do some fun things with Jasmine and Braden. They are overdue for time with their auntie anyway."

"Good, I have a few things I'm going to put in place so both of you have a seat really quick and let me tell you what else I need."

Brandon smiled as they gathered around his desk like the three Musketeers. In a sense, they were because they always had each other's backs and right now, he needed their help more than ever if he was going to do his job at home and remind his wife why he loves her so much.

~~

Brandon entered the house and with each step he took, his feet felt heavier and heavier. He'd been home for less than a day and earlier in the day, he'd walked out after arguing yet again with Dakota and he knew something had to give and the ball was in his court. His brother and sister were right, he wasn't looking at things from Dakota's perspective. All he focused on was being the ultimate provider for his family and what he failed to see and do was be there for his family without focusing on the financial aspect. Today, he actually felt Dakota's disgust with him and he didn't like the way it made him feel.

Not stopping, he headed straight for the steps, happy that he was able to make it home before midnight, though he would have to get up early for a meeting that he knew was too late for him to cancel. Everything else on his calendar for the next few weeks would have to wait and he couldn't wait to surprise Dakota with actions and not just words.

There would be no talking to her tonight so that he could explain the realizations he'd come to, but he knew that it was time to show her and not just make a bunch of promises that she wouldn't trust anyway. Tomorrow was going to be a big day and he was looking forward to seeing the smile on her face that he'd missed seeing lately. With the help of his sister this evening, tomorrow was about to kick off an incredible weekend and he was going to give it his everything. He needed to get his wife back.

After checking in on the kids, he walked into his bedroom and found Dakota fast asleep. Not disturbing her, he went about his usual routine of taking a shower and slipping into bed beside her. He didn't want to wake her, but he did need to feel close to her. Her back was to him, so he slid over and pulled her back against him.

"Baby, are you asleep?" he crooned quietly, not trying to wake her if she was sleeping, but wanting her to hear him if she wasn't sound asleep.

He heard her moan and knew that she was asleep, but still felt his presence in bed with her.

"I'm sorry. I don't know if you're awake enough to hear me, but I'm sorry. I'm sorry about the fight earlier today and for walking out. I'm sorry that I haven't been around the way I know I should be and none of you deserve my absence. I made a promise to you several times before and each time I've gone back on those promises. I won't make them again to have you walk around with false hope. What I will say is that I love you more than anything - I always have and I always will. You, Jasmine and Braden are my life and when my life isn't right and happy then it's up to me to fix it and I will. Don't stop loving me and don't give up on me. Today, I saw a look that said you were fed up and I never want to see that again. Tonight, I want to lay here with you in my arms and I want you to know that I'm here and I always will be. I'll be right here, baby, and I'm not going anywhere."

Brandon wasn't expecting a response knowing she was asleep. He snuggled up against her warm body, kissed her on the back of the shoulder, wrapped his arm around her waist and laid his head on the pillow right behind hers. Feeling at home with her in his arms, he whispered love for her again and again and right before falling off to sleep, he heard her say she loved him too. He smiled as slumber embraced him, but not before he felt Dakota enclose his hand in hers and held on tight before falling back to sleep.

8-Love on Top

After dropping the kids off at camp, Dakota jetted off to the store to get the cupcakes she'd promised she would donate for the afternoon closing exercises. She was thankful for Alisha who had also volunteered to bring healthy fruit snacks for the kids and they were planning to meet back up at the center in time for the program to begin.

She was feeling extra good today as she faintly remembered the night before when Brandon had come home late, but not as late has he had been for the past few months. He'd held her in his arms and apologized for so much that had gone wrong lately, but he wasn't the only one to blame. She had the entire rest of the evening to think about their fight earlier that day and she felt bad about how hard she was being on him. He was trying his best to balance everything in his life and she wasn't being as patient as she could. She was selfishly putting pressure on him and it led to his struggles with doing the right thing in all aspects of his life. She had hoped he would have come home earlier so that they could talk about how they left things, but she was exhausted and after putting the kids to bed early, she went to bed early herself. She wasn't sure what time he'd come in, but when he started talking to her, she opened her eyes briefly and the clock on the night stand said it was just after midnight, which was early for him.

In the morning, she woke up to him kissing her on the lips, again apologizing and telling her he would see her later on. When she finally did wake up, on the other side of the bed sat a dozen bright red roses that were absolutely beautiful. Brandon hadn't given her flowers in a long time and the gesture brought tears to her eyes. She wanted her marriage back, but she didn't want to badger him about it. She resolved that she would stop pressing and complaining and cherish the time they did have. Perhaps she could try and sleep earlier in the evening and not be as tired when he finally did come home. If the only time she got to spend with him was late hours in the middle of the night, then she would make the sacrifice and do her part to make their relationship better.

Picking up her order from the bakery, she was heading back to her car when her cell phone beeped. Placing them solidly in her trunk, she checked her phone and smiled when she saw a message from Brandon telling her how much he loved her. She typed back a response letting him know that she loved him, too and that she was with him one hundred percent, no matter what.

Jumping in her car, she headed back to the camp. She rushed inside and found the table to put the cupcakes on just as the program was about to start. Parents and kids were milling around and she spotted Jasmine and Braden out of the corner of her eye and was surprised to see that they were each smiling up at Brandon.

If she never smiled again, Dakota smiled brighter than she ever had before. He'd made it to the program after she thought that he had a meeting he wouldn't be able to get out of. Making her way over to them, she hugged him the minute he was in reach and whispered in his ear.

"I thought you couldn't make it," she said happily. She knew the kids were beaming that he was there, too.

"No more promises to do better, I'm just going to do it. My kids are more important than any meeting and so I postponed it until later today. I wanted to be here to celebrate their last day of camp. I saw Alisha and she was looking for you saying something about where to put the snacks?" he said.

"I'll find her and find a spot for the snacks. I'm really glad you're here," she said again before walking off.

"I'm glad you're here too, Daddy," Jasmine said.

"I wouldn't miss this for anything. You better get going because it looks like the program is about to start. I'm going to find a seat for me and mommy. I want to get good pictures to share with grandma and grandpa who are mad they couldn't be here."

"I miss grandma and grandpa," Jasmine said.

"I miss them, too," Braden added.

"Well, I'm thinking you and Braden can go and spend a few days with them soon. Would you like that?" he asked them.

"Yes!" they both chimed at the same time.

"Well, let's talk about it later. Right now, go get ready. I see your teacher looking for you," he pointed out.

After the kids ran off to join the others, Brandon looked around for a seat where he could get the best pictures without being disruptive. Just as he was about to sit down, Dakota showed back up and took the seat right next to him just as the program started.

They laughed, sang and clapped throughout the program and Brandon realized how much of the life with his family he had been missing out on. His daughter was a talented dancer and now he saw why Dakota wanted to put her in dance classes, something he was planning on making sure they did. Braden appeared to have a lot of energy that needed to be used in other areas like sports. They needed new ways to allow him to expel that energy and releasing in other ways besides his pre-kindergarten classroom the minute he started school. He'd seen a father of two other kids who had approached him before about helping out with the pee-wee football league and he was planning to have a conversation with him after the program to see if the offer still stood. He would love signing Braden up for active sports and be a part of the coaching staff. These were prime years with his kids and he didn't want to miss anything.

By the end of the program, Brandon had run out of space on his cell phone because he'd taken lots of pictures and videos.

"How did we do?" Jasmine asked when she came running up to him.

"You both did really good. I am proud of you. Mommy went to serve food at the tables. Why don't you go get something to eat and grab Daddy a cupcake while I go over and talk to a few other parents?"

"Okay," Jasmine said, taking Braden by the hand and walking toward the food area. Seeing all of the parents in attendance, Brandon knew that he'd missed out on a lot of gatherings for Jasmine and Braden, but that would end today. He would never have his children longing for his presence at anything they were involved in.

~~

"What did you do to get my brother here?" Alisha

asked.

Dakota looked up from handing out the last of the cupcakes when Alisha sauntered up.

"Nothing. I had no idea he was going to be here. I told you about our blowup yesterday and last night, he came home early and even though I was pretty much asleep, I heard him say he was no longer going to tell me he was going to do better, but that he would just do better. I guess being here today was his start at doing that. I'm not mad at him. Did you see how excited the kids were to see him show up? I was just as happy as they were."

"I could see it all over you and I saw it all over him, too. He was having a good time and not worried about work."

"True. I'm glad he was able to move his meeting to later today. I'm going to take the kids home and relax. Are you still hanging with us this weekend? I still want to take them to that fair tomorrow and spend the day hanging out. I'm going to get them in bed early after dinner, so that we can get an early start tomorrow."

Alisha looked away and tried to act like she was busy. She didn't want to lie to Dakota, but she didn't want to give away what Brandon had planned. His plans were already in motion and the part she played would begin in a few hours, unbeknownst to Dakota. She had to keep up her part of the deal and not let on that something was up. She knew how much it meant to Brandon that everything goes according to his plans.

"Absolutely. I am all in for this weekend," which wasn't really a lie. It was all she was willing to add to the conversation.

"I think I'm going to head out. We'll have a busy day tomorrow and they need downtime this evening. The parents assigned to clean up are already making their way to our table and I don't want to be in the way. What time will you come by in the morning or the kids and I can pick you up?" Dakota asked.

Alisha had to think fast.

"I'll come by your house," she said quickly.

She smiled to herself knowing that statement was true, too, though it would be true for later in the day and not for tomorrow. She was getting more excited about the weekend than Brandon was and Dakota would be.

"I'm going to catch Brandon before he leaves to be sure the kids get hugs and kisses. I'm sure they'll be asleep by the time he gets in. I'll call you later this evening and thanks for helping out today."

"You know I'm always here when you need me, especially for anything involving my niece and nephew that you gave birth to just for me!" she declared.

"That's exactly how it seems sometimes," Dakota said as he smiled and walked away.

She went in search of her family and found Brandon and the kids standing near the entrance.

"Hey, baby!" Brandon said the minute she approached.

"Hey yourself."

"We were just about to go in search of you. I had a great time at the program, but the meeting I pushed ahead is coming up and I need to get going. I hope you're good with that," he said, hoping his mentioning it wouldn't put a damper on the great afternoon they'd just had.

"Not at all. Thank you for being here with us today. I could see from the look on the kids' faces that they loved having you here and so did I. Jasmine beamed every time she looked your way. Will you be late tonight? I was thinking I would wait up for you," she said, hopeful that he would see that she was putting more of an effort in not putting all the work that needed to be done in their marriage on him.

"I won't be late at all and I absolutely want you to wait up for me. Jasmine, take Braden and go say goodbye to Aunt Alisha and Mommy will come right back to get you. Give me a hug and kiss and I'll see you later on. I love you," he exclaimed to them.

"Love you too, daddy," both kids said together and ran off.

"Walk with me," Brandon said and took Dakota by the hand as they walked toward his car. He was about to say something when the father who had approached him about the little league football team walked up.

"Thanks again for agreeing to join our coaching staff this fall and we're looking forward to seeing you and Braden every Saturday. The kids are going to have a good time chasing that ball around the field."

"Marcus, this is my wife, Dakota," Brandon said introducing them. He'd talked to Marcus right after the program and they worked out some details for him to have an active role in the pee-wee league and he was signing Braden up to play.

"Nice to meet you," she said and still feeling a little left out about the conversation they were having about Brandon coaching something and Braden being a part of some team. What had she missed?

"No problem. I'm looking forward to it and I know Braden is going to have a good time. Call my office about the uniforms because I was serious when I said my brother and I will sponsor the team uniforms this year."

"Great. I'll do that first thing Monday morning. Catch you soon, Brandon. Nice to meet you, Dakota."

"Likewise," she said to his departing back.

As soon as they reached Brandon's truck they stopped and he turned around to face her.

"Come here," he said, pulling her into his embrace.

"What was that about?" she asked.

"Oh that? I agreed to join the coaching staff for the pee-wee league football and I'm going to sign Braden up for the team. They start at four years old. Not a lot of contact, but more of just letting them run around the field. I think he'll love it and it will help with that extra energy he has."

Dakota didn't know what to say. Who was this man and where was her extremely busy husband?

"Braden will love it because he'll get to hang more with you. I'm proud of you."

"And I love you. Come closer," he said reaching for her hand and pulling her flush up against his body.

The moment they came in contact, she gasped when she realized she felt something very long and very thick nudging at her center.

"Um, something tells me this isn't the time or place for that so you need to think of something cold, wintery and non-sexual," she laughed.

"I can't. I'm always like this when you're close by. Just don't move or we'll give all the people walking by a show this day camp will never forget," he wisecracked.

"This feels too good to move. Too bad we can't jump in the back seat right quick like we use to do back in our college days."

"Oh, yeah! Those backseat days bring back good, good memories and don't think I won't. All I'm saying is let me call my brother to get bail money together because what I would do to you in that back seat would get us arrested and probably never invited to bring our kids back to this camp again."

They laughed and Brandon loved the sound of her laughter again.

"Okay, no more sex talk or I'm going to tell you to call Aiden to get that money ready," she said.

Brandon leaned down and captured her lips in a kiss she thought was meant to be quick, but it wasn't. When she felt the decent thing would be to pull back, Brandon deepened the kiss and moaned when she opened her mouth and he dived in, dueling with her tongue and mimicking the way he loved to make love to her body, deeply and thoroughly. Forgetting about the fact that they were standing in the middle of a busy parking lot, she joined him in the kiss and reached up until her arms were comfortably around his neck. They were so involved in the intoxicating connection that they barely heard a sound behind them of someone clearing their throat.

"Break it up you two and stop giving these kids a visual of the start to the birds and the bees story," Alisha said behind them.

Dakota pulled away and turned to see her kids trying to look around Alisha to see what they were doing.

"Whew, for a minute, I forgot where we were," she said, reaching up to wipe lipstick from Brandon's lips to remove all signs that they were devouring each other in the parking lot like two teenagers.

"Well, no one else seemed to forget where you were. You're drawing a crowd. I was about to take out my phone to call you a room and send you on your way. The kids are ready?" Alisha said, pointing to the Jasmine and Braden who were safely tucked behind her, out of view of the hot scene before her.

"I'm leaving anyway. I'll see you later. Bye kids," Brandon said and got in his truck.

"Looks like things are looking up in the King household."

"Oh, things are definitely looking up. Let me get the kids home. I'll call you later?" Dakota said walking towards her own car.

"Sounds like a good plan. I have a few things to do and we'll talk later."

Alisha smiled as she walked to her car, taking out her phone to call her brother to be sure he had everything planned out. Dakota was about to get the shock of her life and she already knew it would be a shock of the best kind.

9-Love on Top

"Mommy, can we have pizza for dinner tonight?" Jasmine asked.

Dakota's mind was flooded with the hot kiss Brandon had given her at the camp. She couldn't wait to stay awake for a sexy night with him. The way he felt all hard and ready when she leaned into him at his car overwhelmed her and she couldn't wait until she could feel the real thing, skin to skin. She'd missed him and it was clear he was missing her, too.

"You just had all those snacks at camp and you're already thinking about pizza?" she asked as they pulled up to the house.

"No, not pizza right now, but in a little while. We still have to have dinner and you said if we did a good job at the camp program today, we could have pizza tonight."

Her kids never forgot anything, especially when she made them a promise about something they really love and they both loved pizza.

"Yes, you can have pizza tonight."

"Can we have French fries too?" Braden asked.

Dakota looked over her shoulder at them and all she saw was teeth smiling back at her. She never could resist giving in to them.

"Yes, French fries, too. I'll order everything after everyone has had a bath and in pajamas in a few hours. How is that?"

She smiled brighter when Braden and Jasmine both chimed in agreement.

Pulling into her driveway, she raised the garage door and as soon as she parked, she opened the door for the kids who both ran past her into the house through the garage door that led into the kitchen. Following quickly behind them, she locked the door and searched around for the pile of menus that were kept in the kitchen drawer. Within seconds, she could hear the television turn on in the family room and knew that for the moment, the kids would be engaged in whatever was on the Disney Network.

She took a moment to run up to her bedroom and thought about having something sexy on when Brandon came home. She knew it would probably be really late, but she didn't care. Their love was worth it and if it was the wee hours of the morning when they could find time to bond again, so be it.

She dug around in her closet and found a cute, sexy black nightie that she knew he loved seeing her in. Laying it out on the bed, she would prepare for her night after putting the kids down. Going back down to check on the them, she sat down and relaxed with them for a while as she anxiously awaited the arrival of Brandon later that night.

After an hour of Disney cartoons, Dakota couldn't take anymore and remembering she forgot to grab the mail, she got up to go to the mailbox.

"I'm going to run out to the mailbox to get the mail, so don't either of you move until I get back. Jasmine, you're in charge."

Dakota smiled when she heard Jasmine cheer while Braden moaned.

"Don't pout, Braden. I'm the oldest and that's why I'm in charge," Jasmine said.

"Be nice, Jasmine," Dakota said as she walked to the door.

Pulling it open, she was startled to see that there were people on the other side of the door. Recognizing her sister-in-law, she waited while her heart rate slowed down.

"Hey sis!" Alisha said.

"Don't hey sis me – you scared me."

"Oh, I'm sorry. I was about to ring the bell when the door suddenly opened."

Looking to the man standing next to her sister-in-law, dressed like a funeral director, she looked at Alisha questionably.

"You brought someone with you? Where's Chris?" she asked.

"Chris is in Chicago, remember? He'll be back on Monday. This is Thomas and he's the guy driving that long white limousine that's sitting in front of your house."

Dakota was so focused on the two of them that she hadn't noticed a limousine parked out front. Looking beyond them, she saw the long, stretched white limousine and gasped at its beauty.

"Wow! Why in the world did you show up here in a limousine? What's going on?" Dakota asked.

"Oh, he's not here for me, he's here for you," Alisha said.

"For me? Why?"

Before she could ask any more questions, Alisha handed her an envelope.

"This letter is for you and I'm here to pick up the kids for the weekend? Are you going to let me in or are we going to keep standing here at the door as if you don't know me?" Alisha said smiling and walking around Dakota into the house.

"What's this letter?" she asked.

"Don't open it yet. Thomas, you can wait for Dakota at the limousine and she'll be out shortly."

Dakota looked from Alisha to Thomas as he walked away feeling like she was in an episode of The Twilight Zone. She had no clue what was happening."

"Where are my babies!" Alisha yelled and within

seconds, Jasmine and Braden came running and jumped on her as they all fell to the floor.

One thing was for sure and that was Jasmine and Braden loved their aunt who spoiled them rotten.

"Okay guys, let Aunt Alisha up off of the floor so that she can tell me what's going on."

"That letter is what's going on and as soon as I get the kids, their sleeping bags and enough clothes for a weekend at my house, you can open it, but not until then."

"What is with the mystery? You're taking the kids for the weekend? We have plans for tomorrow, remember?" Dakota asked, not really intrigued.

"I have plans with them tomorrow, you no longer do. Okay, kids, how about you spend the weekend with Aunt Alisha?"

Dakota watched the scene unfold before her and felt like she was on the outside looking in.

"Yeah!" both kids yelled at the same time.

"Good and we're going to have a lot of fun."

"Can we have pizza and French fries? Mommy was going to order some for delivery and also some chicken nuggets," Braden said.

"That's all? I can top that. I say we get pizza, French fries, chicken nuggets and also get some ice cream! How does that sound?" Alisha said.

"Yeah!" the kids shouted again.

"Alisha?"

"Let's go to your rooms and pack a lot of clothes,

enough for a few days and I'll go to the garage and look for your sleeping bags and don't forget clean underclothes. We forgot last time and I had to buy all new undies."

As the kids ran for the steps, Dakota watched Alisha as she headed for the garage with her following close behind, still bewildered. Alisha showed up like a steamroller and mowed her down with no explanation, leaving her wondering what was going on.

"Alisha?" she called after her.

"Are their sleeping bags still in the garage? They were there after our last sleepover."

"Alisha!" Dakota said again, trying to get her attention.

"I also need to borrow Brandon's tent. I think I'm going to set up the tent in my family room and we can pretend we're having a sleepover outside."

"Alisha! Are you losing your mind? Don't you hear me talking to you? Why are you here kidnapping my kids for an entire weekend and why is there a limousine with a driver sitting in front of my house? I'm going to keep adding more questions on until you answer a few," she said.

Alisha turned and faced her.

"Go with this okay. I'm going to give you a break from the kids this weekend and spend some quality time with them especially since Chris is out of town. I could use the company since I didn't have much else planned. As for you, do like I said and as soon as the kids and I leave, read the letter and all will be answered. You trust me, I know you do, so there is nothing to worry about. Read the letter. Now, do me a favor and pull out the sleeping bags and Brandon's camping tent while I go up and help the kids get their things together. Nothing crazy is going on, just get ready to enjoy your weekend and no more questions. The letter will answer every question you have floating around in that head of yours. I will be around Monday to drop the kids off and you can thank me then," Alisha smiled and walked away.

"I'll be thanking you on Monday?" Dakota asked.

Alisha turned around and had a grin that said something was afoot and she knew all about it.

"Oh yes – you will be thanking me on Monday, trust me."

With that, she watched Alisha disappear up the stairs and she went further into the garage and pulled out the kids' sleeping bags and located Brandon's tent. Opening the garage door, she saw Alisha's truck in the driveway and checking to be sure the door was opened, and it was, she placed everything in the back along with the kids' booster seats from the back of her car and went back into the house, still holding on to the letter. She was tempted to open it, but she'd do like Alisha asked and wait until she and the kids left.

Going into the family room to turn the television off, she heard the sound of kids running down the stairs and she went back out to the front door to greet them.

"You have fun and do what Aunt Alisha says, okay?" she said to them.

Before either could answer, Jasmine opened the door and she and Braden ran out to Alisha's truck.

"I guess they're ready for a break too, huh?" Alisha quipped.

"I guess they are. Can I at least get a hug and kiss?" Dakota yelled to them before they got up in the truck.

Followed by Braden, Jasmine ran back to her, hugged her tightly, before they both waved and ran back to the truck, clearly ready to go.

"Bye mommy!" they both yelled and closed the truck door behind them.

"Well, I guess they're ready for a weekend with you."

"That's because I told them about all the fun we're going to have and they're excited. Now, I have one demand and that is, do not call me to check on them and I mean don't call even once. Read your letter and when you're ready, Thomas will be right here waiting for you. Enjoy yourself and let any and everything go that has been weighing on you lately. Allow yourself to live in the moment and get back what life has been trying to steal from you. Deal?" Alisha asked.

Dakota didn't know what was going on, but Alisha was like the sister she didn't have and she trusted her with any and every thing. Holding tightly to the letter, she gave Alisha a hug.

"Deal," she whispered.

"Good, now have fun and we'll talk to you on Monday and not before then. I'll drop them off after giving them dinner. Love you, sis!"

"Love you, too!" Dakota said to Alisha's back as she rushed to her truck, got in and backed out of the driveway.

Dakota waved wildly to the kids who were waving back at her. Once they were out of sight, her eyes turned to Thomas who was standing at the curb at the door to the limousine apparently waiting on her. She smiled at him and retreated back into the house to read her letter.

Opening the envelope that had her name typed out on the front, she opened the letter and began to read as she walked toward the stairs that led to her bedroom.

"Hi, baby. I know this is all catching you by surprise and you have no clue what's going on, but that's how I wanted this to be. We have spent so much time fighting and arguing lately that I realized we were in dire need of some "us" time. I'm sorry for not realizing the importance of my time spent with you and the kids and if that in any way made you feel anything less than wanted by me, then I am truly sorry for my error in judgement over deciding what's most important to me. I love you more than life itself. I love you as

much today as I did the very first time I told you that I loved you. You are more beautiful with each passing day and I never want you to forget how much you mean to me and how incredibly sexy and desirable you are. I haven't done the best job at showing you how much you mean to me and how much I love you. Sometimes, it gets easy to say the words, but it's the showing you that I need to hone up on. It was time I took a step back and showed you that you are my everything – you always have been and always will be. I have something special planned for us this weekend and I want it to be about you and me and nothing else. Thanks to my sister, who always comes through in a pinch, she's going to spend a weekend of fun with the kids, giving you and I the time together that I know we need. What I need you to do is pack enough clothes for yourself for the weekend because we're not coming back to the house until Monday morning. Make sure you pack something hot and sexy for you to wear for you and something hotter and sexier for you to wear just for me. Don't worry about anything for me because I have that covered. The theme for the weekend is love. It's about the love we felt that night we first made love, to that day when we said "I do" and that moment when you told me for the first time that you were pregnant with our first child. This weekend I want to give you all of me the way I promised you I always would, but somehow *lately, I've forgotten that. I love you, Dakota, and I always have been, am and always will be yours! After you have everything, Thomas has instructions on where to take you and when you get to your destination, they'll be other instructions. Get ready for a weekend that will be about nothing, but you and me. Love, Brandon.*

Dakota didn't realize she'd been crying while reading the letter until a tear smeared the typed print of the letter.

Excitement flowed through her as she thought about an entire weekend of nothing, but her and Brandon finding their way back to each other. Without second guessing anything, she headed into their bedroom and immediately went in search of the bag that she'd tucked in the back of her walk-in closet.

On a shopping trip a few weeks ago with Alisha, she'd brought a sexy red set and because they had been arguing so much lately, she had put the bag in her closet and never thought about it again. She knew it was time to pull it out and wow her husband.

The day she'd bought the sexy lingerie, she questioned whether she should get it or not because she had begun to feel self-conscious about how her body had changed after giving birth to two children. She remembered sharing with Alisha how she wasn't sure Brandon found her sexy anymore because the intimacy had been a casualty of his busy work schedule.

Putting any reservations to the side, her husband wanted a hot, sexy weekend with her and she was planning on putting all of her negative thoughts away and only focus on them and only them this weekend. Getting what she needed from the bag, she pulled out one of her suitcases from her closet and began searching through her clothes for what she would need for the weekend. After adding toiletries, jewelry and other essential items, she disrobed and hopped in the shower. She had a weekend of love to get ready for and if Brandon wasn't quite ready for her, he would be because ready or not, here she comes.

10-Love on Top

Brandon wrapped up his last meeting and despite all of the opposition from his crew and his staff at the nightclub, he was walking out of the door after giving strict instructions that no one was to contact him for anything at all. If there were any issues, all calls should be directed to Aiden and no one would be hearing from him until Tuesday at the earliest. He smiled at all of the looks of shock he saw on the many faces who didn't believe he was disconnecting from everything for an entire weekend, something he had never done before. This was a first for them and all at once, everyone started bombarding him with one question after another as if he was never coming back.

"Listen, I promise this place will not crumble because I'm not here and construction on the new location will continue in my absence. Everything business related can go through Aiden until I return and anything else, I don't want to know about anyway, so save it for another time. I'm out of here and I mean it when I say don't contact me. Anyone who attempts is going to be fired!" he yelled and laughed.

Brandon knew he didn't really mean that he would fire anybody, but he wanted them to know how serious he was about not being contacted for any reason. He wanted to focus on Dakota this weekend and nothing else. With his kids in the hands of his sister, he didn't have a care in the world and for the next few days, nothing else mattered, knowing they would be safe and knowing that he would have an entire weekend to remind his wife of why he fell in love with her and never stopped.

"What if there is a serious emergency and we can't locate Aiden?" one employee asked.

"Suppose someone comes in and says they will only deal with you and no one else?" yet another employee said.

"What about scheduling for the rest of the weekend? You know everyone will try and get over on Aiden."

"Is that so?" Aiden asked entering the room just as his name was mentioned.

That same employee tried to backtrack on his words.

"I didn't mean it like that," he said and then

quieted down.

"Like Brandon said, he is not to be contacted for any reason about anything at all. Any issues, questions or concerns, feel free to let me know. I will be here the entire weekend and it's business as usual. I know you're used to dealing with Brandon, but not this weekend. I'm all you have and I advise you to tread lightly," he said and grinned as the crowd laughed.

"I'm out of here. I have plans and other than a natural disaster, nothing is going to keep me from them. No contact, Aiden," he said as he walked toward the exit.

"I got you, no contact. Don't hurt anything this weekend," he jested at Brandon knowing he was planning a weekend of love with his wife.

Brandon laughed out loud.

"You should tell Dakota that. I haven't been the most attentive husband lately and we're overdue. There is no telling how much she has stored up for me. She may break a brother in half," he laughed.

"Tell her to go easy on you as you promise to never neglect her like this again and maybe, just maybe she'll cut you some slack. You know I could use another niece or nephew," Aiden laughed.

Brandon didn't answer. If it were up to him, he'd have a half-dozen kids running around, but it wasn't solely up to him. The first thing on his agenda was to fix his marriage before talking about having any more kids. He had become distant lately, leaving Dakota to take care of the kids alone most of the time and that didn't bode well for his desire for more children. Checking the time, he had just enough time to get home, shower, change and pack clothes for the weekend. He'd already received a call from Alisha that she had the kids with her and was headed home. Thomas had also sent him a text that Dakota was safely tucked into the back of the limousine and he was driving her to the appointed destination.

Jogging to his truck, he couldn't wait to get his hands, his arms and every other body part on his sexy wife and before the end of the weekend, he knew there would be no residue of negativity about his love and commitment to her remaining.

~~

Dakota was nervous as if she'd never had a romantic evening with her husband before. After finally getting her bags packed for the weekend, she exited her house to find Thomas still standing in the same place. As she got closer, he walked ahead and took her luggage from her, placing it in the back and then opening the door for her to get in. Once inside, she was greeted with another lovely, yet sexy note from Brandon followed by another dozen of red roses. There was also a small black velvet box with a bright red bow tied around it with a little note that said, "open me" on the top. She opened it and inside was an exquisite diamond tennis bracelet, one that she had been looking at months ago when they had gone out to dinner and stopped by a jewelry store. The note inside of the box simply said, "beautiful diamonds for my beautiful wife, I love you, Brandon".

Taking the bracelet out of the box, it took her a few minutes, but she was able to finally get the bracelet clasped tightly and it looked amazing on her wrist. Brandon was outdoing himself and if this was only the beginning, she wondered if she'd survive a weekend or even a night of surprises from him. Now, she wondered where they were going. She wanted to ask Thomas, but decided to let the night continue to fill with surprises the way Brandon planned for it to be.

After driving along for what seemed an eternity, they pulled up in front of a place called *The Fisher Island Club* and to say it was beautiful would be an understatement. She'd heard that the club was one of the nicest around and guests were treated like royalty. Once the limousine stopped, she waited for Thomas to come around and open her door. He did so with her luggage in hand as a woman exited the entrance of the club and greeted her.

"Good evening, Mrs. King. I'm Phoebe and I'm your host for the weekend. I am on call all day and night to provide any and everything you need while you're staying with us. The phone in you room dials me directly and as soon as you pick it up, it will ring my cell phone. Anything at all that I can do to make your stay a grand one, let me know. I'll have someone take your bags up to your suite and everything at the request of your husband has been set up for you. I'll escort you up to your room to familiarize you with all of the amenities and then if there is anything at all that I can get you or do for you, call me anytime."

"Thank you, Phoebe. Is my husband here yet?" she asked.

"Not yet. He did ask me to give him a ring once you arrived and were escorted to your suite. I will do that the moment I return to my office after I know that I have answered all of your questions and you're satisfied with the suite. Is that okay?" she asked.

"Yes, it is. Looks like my husband thought of everything."

"Yes, he did and he made it clear – only the best for you and he expects you to have the kind of treatment like we've never given another customer before, which is why I'm available to you around the clock. No matter how big or small your need is, call me."

"I will and thank you."

Dakota road up in the elevator barely able to contain her excitement for what was in store for the evening. Phoebe continued explaining to her all that the club had to offer. She heard her talking, but her mind turned to how excited she was that Brandon had pulled this all together and she knew nothing about it. When did he do all of this, she wondered? With no doubt in her mind, she was embracing whatever their time together this weekend would bring because he took the time to plan it out and she was riding with it all the way.

11 Love on Top

Brandon pulled up to *The Fisher Island Club*, a spot a friend of his recommended for a nice, quiet and local getaway. What he really wanted to do was whisk his wife away to a tropical island, but he's holding out on doing that until after his plans for next week to take the family on a much-needed getaway. Following that, he and Dakota were going to get away to an island and make love underneath a starry night where he wanted to continue to stoke the fires of their loving marriage. Never again would he put anything, especially business, before her and his children. Handing his keys to the valet who approached, he was greeted by a woman he assumed was Phoebe, the person he'd been planning their weekend with.

"Hello, Mr. King."

"Phoebe, good to see you. Is my wife all settled in?" he asked.

"Yes, she is. I have everything set up in the room

just like you asked and the final details of your dinner are being handled right now. Do you still want it delivered in an hour?"

"An hour is good. Please make sure someone calls to let me know that they're on their way."

"Will do."

As they walked, Phoebe handed him an envelope.

"I appreciate you helping with everything," Brandon said.

"It's my pleasure. Now, inside the envelope is your room key and other contact information you'll need for the weekend. Let me run a few more things by you about the other accommodations you asked me to take care of."

"Did everything pan out?" he asked, hopeful.

"Yes, and I was able to confirm that all of your arrangements are as you requested."

Brandon felt like he wanted to jump up and click his heels with excitement over the romantic weekend he'd prepared for his love. He listened as Phoebe gave him the rest of the confirmed details while they walked.

~~

Dakota walked around the suite and took in everything about it. There were flowers everywhere and champagne was chilling on ice. There was a small fire in the fireplace with a large fur rug spread out in front of it. At the edge of the rug were trays of chocolate candy covered in clear containers.

Walking to the bedroom, the bed was covered in rose petals and some were strewn out on the floor. There were his and her towels spread out along a seat in the master bathroom where oils and soaps along with candles lined the outer edge of the jacuzzi which was inviting. They had one at home, but this one was heavenly and she couldn't wait to get in it. She had already unpacked her clothes and put them away and once she arrived at the suite, she changed clothes and put on a small black dress that she knew drove Brandon wild and underneath, she had on something special just for him. She was anxious for him to arrive. She was on cloud nine.

~~

Brandon opened the door to their suite and his heart rate sped up the moment he saw Dakota looking lovely on the other side. Closing the door behind him, he smiled the moment she turned and smiled at him. Neither moved, but stared as if they were seeing each other for the first time.

"Hi, baby! You look amazing," he crooned in the sexiest voice he could make.

She was the most incredible sight he'd ever seen and he took his time caressing her with his eyes from her head, where she had her long hair pulled up into a tight ponytail on the top of her head all the way to her feet which were encased in high heels and the one thing he loved was watching her walk in them. There was something about women in heels that turned him on, especially when that woman was his wife.

As he continued to peruse her gorgeousness, he noticed she was wearing a dress that was a favorite of his, a little black one that hugged her delectable body in all the right places. Without thinking of his next action as a result of what he was seeing, he snaked his tongue out and licked his lips the moment he saw the deep cleavage cut of the dress that showed just enough of her luscious mounds, enough to get his body's temperate rising quickly. He knew his boxer briefs were going to be a problem for most of the evening if he didn't soon get them both naked. Knowing he had all night, he pushed thoughts out of his mind of her gorgeous body laid out for his taking and focused more on the fact that they were going to spend an entire weekend, starting tonight, focusing on nothing, but each other.

"You look pretty good yourself. When did you have time to change?" she asked, walking toward him slowly.

"After I knew you were on your way here in the limousine where Thomas was instructed to drive you very slowly I might add, I went to the house, changed and grabbed what I would need for this weekend that will be all about our love."

"Thank you for doing this. I haven't been this excited in a very long time."

"You'll never have to wait to be this excited ever again."

This weekend was going to be about reassuring her of his want and need for her in all aspects of his life.

Walking to meet her halfway, he could tell she was about to say something else, but her lips were calling to him. She had on light makeup and he could see a sheen coating on her lips that called out to him and he could no more resist tasting them than he could keep himself from taking his next breath. Lightly pulling her to him, he held her body close to his and leaned in for a sweet kiss on her lips. He first kissed one corner and he felt her body shiver.

"I've been waiting to do this since the moment I knew you were on your way here," he whispered against her lips.

He then moved to the other side and kissed the other corner of her lips. Dakota exhaled and he knew that meant she was rising to the occasion. Just as she opened her mouth to respond, he took that moment to search out her tongue and as their lips locked, he kissed her long and hard. He reveled in how she tasted sweet and sugary and his mouth exploded in delight. His heart felt like it was beating on the outside of his chest as it swelled with uncontainable love for her. When he finally pulled back, he had to slow his breathing in order to speak again. He could tell from how deeply Dakota was breathing that she was having the same struggles. That was one powerful kiss.

"Wow," she said first.

"Wow is right. I needed that kiss more than you know."

Dakota smiled up at him where even in heels, he was still several inches taller.

"I know I sure did and your kisses never disappoint."

"So, what do you think so far about the start to our weekend?" he asked.

"I've been waiting to hear how you were able to pull this off," she said as he walked her toward the table where a nice bottle of champagne was on ice waiting for them.

"Would you like a glass?" he asked.

"Yes," Dakota said not taking her eyes off of him.

While Brandon poured them each a glass, he watched her take in the ambience of the room.

"Do you like it?"

"I love it. I've heard about this place, but I had no idea the suites were this beautiful. I wonder if the rooms are always filled with this many floral arrangements. They are lovely."

"I don't know what the rooms usually look like, but I had all these arrangements ordered just for you. I know how much you love flowers and I haven't been giving you enough of them lately, not like I have in the past. For a while now, I've forgotten about what's important, but not anymore."

"I know you love me, Brandon. I think I was

missing you and it made me question the validity of the strength of our bond and I should never have done that. I knew better than to doubt anything about our love."

He handed her a glass of champagne and they sipped.

"This is good," he said.

"It is and it's been a while since I've had champagne."

"You know, you had every right to question me and get us back to where we needed to be. I'd lost focus for a minute and because of the incredible woman I married, I'm grateful that you saw the signs and reigned things back in. That's why our love is strong through anything and our marriage will forever be solid."

Dakota kiss him softly on the lips.

"Yes, it is and it always will be. Now, what are the plans for the weekend?" she asked.

"Baby, this weekend is all about whatever you want to do. I have a few things on standby, but I want to hear what you want to do. We live in Miami, one of the greatest entertainment cities and we have only scratched the surface of tapping into the fun. Now, tonight, I thought we'd stay in, talk, eat and enjoy time with just me and you and most importantly spending all evening and all night making love because baby, we are overdue for some wild times."

"Mmm, that's what I'm talking about. I have

something special for you for tonight," Dakota said, appreciating the fact that he had no idea what was in store for him and hoping that the thought that she was going to make his night as much as he had laid out plans to make hers, she felt powerful.

"Is that so?" he said moving closer to her.

"You'll have to wait for it though," she added.

"Why can't I have it right now? I promise to be a really, really bad boy for you."

Brandon leaned over and licked a path across her exposed cleavage, knowing how much she loved him as a bad, bad boy and he was more than ready to oblige.

"We have all night, right?" she asked, adding a tone to her voice that made her sound like a seductress.

"Yes, we do, but you know how impatient I can be."

"Well, it will be a treat that I believe you'll appreciate at the right time."

Brandon was about to beg and plead when the phone to the suite rang, interrupting their hot scene that was better than some of the scenes in those romance movies she forced him to watch sometimes.

"Hold that thought and I want to come back to this discussion. I can be quite persuasive when I'm begging," he confessed.

Dakota laughed out loud as he ran to grab the phone. She had a feeling tonight was going to be more fun than she could have anticipated. Alisha had the kids for the weekend and she was going to have her sexy ass husband to herself and she had a lot she'd like to re-introduce him to.

"Oh, I love it when you beg," she retorted.

"Hello?" Brandon said answering the phone.

"Mr. King, your dinner is ready and this is the time you asked us to deliver it. Would you like it brought up to your suite now?" Phoebe asked.

"Yes, dinner now would be great and can you also have them bring up the dessert. I'd like to make sure we're not interrupted after dinner is delivered," he said.

"Absolutely. Everything is on its way up and should arrive shortly. If you need anything else this evening, just pick up the phone and you'll be connected to me immediately."

"Thank you, Phoebe."

"You're welcome, Mr. King."

Brandon hung up and turned to Dakota.

"Well, I'll have to work on my begging in my mind for a bit since dinner is on its way up, but trust me, you won't be able to hold out when I put my mack-daddy smile on you. I know just the right words to make you give in to me."

"I can't wait for you to try!" Dakota exclaimed.

"I know we're both dressed for dinner as if we were going out, so if you want to get comfortable, go ahead and do that. We're not leaving this suite tonight."

"I kind of like how dressed up we are and I'm good. I am hungry. I was just about to order pizza for me and the kids when Thomas arrived with the limousine. What are we having?"

Brandon was about to answer when there was a knock at the door.

"Saved by the knock. I'll let you set your eyes on this feast yourself," he said, happy with himself that he had put all of this in place, including a dinner menu that included a lot of her favorites.

Opening the door, he stood to the side as two men rolled in two carts with several covered dishes on them.

"Would you like for us to uncover your meals, sir?" one guy asked.

"No, that won't be necessary."

Brandon reached in his pocket and pulled out two, one-hundred-dollar bills and tipped them and the look on their faces said they were more than appreciative of the gesture. After they left, Dakota joined him at the carts.

"How many people are we feeding?" she asked, noticing both carts were full on both shelves with covered dishes.

Brandon started removing lids to let her see what was underneath each.

"Well, we have a tray of fresh fruit that I thought we'd nibble on all evening and tomorrow. There is a full refrigerator on the other side of that wall," he pointed in the direction of the wall opposite them.

"You know how much I love fruit," she said.

"I know your likes and dislikes, baby," he said smiling.

"What else?"

"Okay, well we have fresh Maryland crab balls and shrimp cocktails as appetizers. Over here we have your favorite, broiled stuffed salmon, with garlic red-skinned potatoes and fresh green beans. For me, you know I need a man's meal, so I have a steak with the same red-skinned potatoes and green beans. We also have French onion soup, salads, garden and Greek and a large tray of cheeses, meats and crackers. Then finally on the bottom here, we have five different kinds of desserts and by my special request, a can of whipped cream and we both know that's not just for the desserts on the tray," he said in a tempting way, letting her garner the direction of his thoughts without actually saying it.

"Well, I hope it's a full can because I have some ideas of my own," Dakota said and reached for the fruit on the tray.

"Is it sweet?" he asked.

"It's very sweet – not as sweet as me, but it's a close second."

Brandon groaned as his body hardened instantly at the thought of all that sweetness between her legs and he was ready to put dinner aside until later and dive into her sweetness now.

"I'm ready to try both and eat dinner later!" he

exclaimed and made a move to reach for her.

"Down, baby. Dinner first and dessert of any kind you like after. Deal?"

Dakota laughed at her husband and at the same time loved how insatiable he was for her. It was taking every bit of strength in her to hold off on devouring him.

"That's a deal. Let's move everything to the table."

Brandon was thankful for the work Phoebe had gone through to have the room set up for his weekend of seduction for his wife. The table had been set up with all the makings for a romantic dinner that included not only candles, but red and white rose pedals spread across the table. Per his request, he knew the bed was covered in them as well and he couldn't wait to get to that room later.

Turning on soft music, he held out her chair before taking the one across from her.

"Everything is nice and these crab balls are delicious. Reminds me of all those days I would visit you and we'd drive into Baltimore for the best seafood around. I wasn't expecting them to be just as good, but they are."

"That's because I had these made at the supper club and sent here. There isn't a better chef around than the ones we hired and the one at the first club is from Baltimore, so he knows all of the secrets including how to use Old Bay seasoning like you like. I got you covered, baby."

When Dakota smiled, Brian felt like the biggest man in the world. She made him feel that way with everything he does. He has only come as far as he has because of the woman sitting across from him.

"Well, he put his foot in these and this salmon is to die for. It's cooked just right. Tell me about some of these other plans you have for us this weekend."

"Tomorrow, I rented a motor yacht and it comes with a captain and two other crew members to cater to you all day long. We'll lay out and relax and I can eye that behind in a sexy bathing suit all day. We can swim, have lunch and an early dinner and relax without a care in the world. That night if we're not completely exhausted, we're going dancing to some sexy Latin music. I want to hold you close and watch those hips tantalize me. How does that sound?"

"Sounds like the perfect day."

"I plan to make this entire weekend as close to perfection as possible and it's because you deserve it, we deserve it and I love you."

As they ate, Brandon loved being able to catch up on all that he'd been missing out on because he'd been so focused on work.

"Are we really going to spend an entire weekend away from the kids?" Dakota asked as they were finishing up dinner.

"I told Alisha to let them call us if they were missing us and anytime you want to check in on them, go ahead. This weekend is about whatever you want to do."

"What about other things you want to do? Where do they fit in?"

Brandon stood up and came around to her side of the table, leaning down to nuzzle her neck.

"Right now, I want to dance with my beautiful wife. That's a good start to getting what I want," he said pulling her chair back to help her stand.

Pulling her into his arms, they moved fluidly around the room, focusing on the smooth jazz sounds and the essence that love was in the air. This, Brandon thought, is what he should have been doing all along.

12 Love on Top

"Thank you for planning all of this for us. I don't know what to say, I'm still in shock. The limousine ride, Alisha scooping up the kids, the suite, the other activities and this night of romance is everything."

"It is and it's everything we need right now; just me and you and reconnecting."

Brandon meant every word because they were way overdue for a weekend like this.

"You've done all of this for me and because it's a surprise, I didn't have a chance to get you anything special," she said, holding on tight where her hands were clasped behind his head as they moved together. Their bodies swayed and moved in a motion that was as smooth as their actions in bed.

"You didn't have to get me anything because this weekend is all about you, baby."

Dakota leaned back and remembered she did have something for him.

"Well, I do have a little something for you to add to our weekend."

"You do."

"I do."

"When do I get it."

"When do you want it?"

"Baby, if you have something for me, I want it right now."

"Are you sure you want it right now?" she asked while moving out of his embrace.

The fact that they were no longer holding on to each other didn't keep her from swaying to the music, enticing him with the soft, silky moves of her hips. She could tell he was completely focused on her because his eyes went from her face straight to her waist and behind the moment she turned around and bent over while still moving her hips around in circles.

"You're killing me, Dakota," he murmured.

"Not yet, you still have to get your surprise."

While her back was to him, she slid the zipper down which was hidden on the side of her dress, starting under her arm. With slow precision, she slid the zipper down and watched the moment he realized what his surprise was. When her dress fell away, she let it drop to the floor and with her back to him, she stood, still in her five-inch stiletto heels and now he could see what her dress had been covering.

"Damn! You've been wearing that sitting across

from me at dinner all night and you're just showing me? If I had known, that dinner would have been ice cold by now."

Brandon moved swiftly in her direction, but she turned and held him off.

"Are you in a rush, big boy?" she asked as she eyed the tent that had grown in the crotch of his pants. He never failed when it came to rising to pleasure her.

"You have no idea how much I want you right now and I'm not only talking about the obvious sign that could probably been seen from space," he joked pointing in the direction of his massive hard-on.

"Oh, I can imagine because I want you like I never have before. Now, if you follow me into the bedroom and you're a really good, bad boy, I'll let you unwrap your present as soon as you're not wearing all of those clothes," she said, sauntering into the bedroom adding an extra swing to her hips, knowing the thong panties gave him a full view of her round backside.

"You know if for any reason I have a heart attack because I'm not sure my heart can stand all of your deliciousness in that red, make sure I'm not discovered with my briefs down around my ankles, like now."

Dakota turned around and almost choked when she saw him standing before her with his pants and boxer briefs down around his ankles. He was a sight that made her chuckle even harder. A few seconds ago, he was fully dressed. She had a hard time controlling her laughter.

"How did you drop your pants and boxers so fast. A second ago, I was looking at you fully clothed," she said as she seductively turned and climbed up on the bed, making sure to move as slow as possible giving him a clear view of what he was about to get. She now knew getting this sexy set was a great idea because she could practically see Brandon foaming at the mouth.

"All I have to think about is you and I'm ready to get naked anytime and anywhere. I'm barely holding on here, already on the brink of a wet dream kind of release," he said pointing to his manhood that was prominently displayed and pointing in her direction.

"Well, maybe I can help you with that," she said and used her finger to signal for him to come closer as she laid back with her head on the pillow and her legs spread wide open. She reached down to remove her heels and he stopped her.

"Don't you take off a thing, especially those heels. I'm thinking I'd like to see you walking around in those all weekend. You have no idea how sexy you are when you walk in high-heels."

Brandon removed the rest of his clothes and climbed up on the bed until his face was level with hers.

Dakota looked into his eyes and he knew that the

unbridled admiration she saw there told her everything he was feeling for her.

Dakota was speechless. Brandon was looking at her the way he had so many times in the past, but this time it was a little different. He had a pleading in his eyes that said he was begging her to read his mind and know that she was his everything. She could see it and she felt it in the aura around them. The moment he leaned down and captured her lips, her sex clenched and she could feel moisture as her body armed for readiness for him.

Brandon positioned his erection in between her legs and moved his hips in a motion that made her wish he would enter her with no pretense because she was ready.

As they kiss, she reached up and held on to both sides of his face and as he moaned her name and told her how much he loved her, how sexy he found her and how he could barely hold off on entering her waiting body, she reached down and brought his hips even closer, encouraging him to not wait.

"We have all weekend for foreplay and slow love making, but right now, I need you," she pleaded.

Brandon reached down and slid her panties off and used his teeth to unclasp the snap at the front of her bra that was keeping him from allowing his eyes to feast on her large mounds. When the cups fell away, he leaned down and caressed first one nipple and then the other with his tongue. He went between the two delighting when the tips pebbled hard under his opened-mouth kisses. His web of desire for her was unmatched to any other time that he could remember and as he nibbled at her skin and heard her say his name again and again, he didn't make either of them wait.

Coming up on his knees, he spread her legs open and before joining their bodies, he slid down until his face was right at that part of her that smelled like heated desire and need for him. He had to have a taste if he did nothing else for the rest of the night.

Going down, he placed his tongue on the silkiness that greeted him and the moment he heard Dakota exhale, he dove in with his tongue, drawing from her everything that had his flesh burning for her. He lapped at her as her hips grinded up into his face. He lifted his head briefly and seeing the hooded gaze of passion that said she was close, he dove back in and this time, he went at her like a starving man until she finally screamed and let go, freeing her body of the pent-up anxiety over any issues they'd been having. It was all gone and left was the woman he wanted to always see, one that knew how desirable she was and always would be.

Sliding up her body, he kissed his way from her stomach, stopping again to pay homage to her lovely breasts and taking her lips, he held her legs wide as he slid inside of her, enjoying the tight glove feeling of her womanhood embracing and caressing him.

"Mine, baby. Now and forever – mine," he said as he began to move. Scooping his hands under her behind to give him even greater penetration, he moved swifter as she cried out for more and more and he gave it to her.

In a cauldron of passion and fiery heat, he pushed all the way into Dakota and together they shattered into a mindless sexy haze that hovered above them with the intent to never let them go. Brandon knew he didn't want to be released; he wanted to stay like this forever, loving Dakota for all perpetuity.

Dakota wasn't sure she was still on earth as her body convulsed with an orgasm that was on the brink of making her pass out. The world exploded in her head, matching the explosions that were wracking through her body. The onslaught of his caresses and strokes in and out of her body, paired with the sounds in the room of their lovemaking sent her crashing again and again into a bliss of never ending waves of delight. Her body wasn't her own and from the beginning, she's always known that it belonged to Brandon because he knew how to please her beyond any level of her expectation. Everything around them dropped away and left in the space was just her and the man she loved more than life itself. At the moment, nothing and no one else needed to be - they just needed each other.

"I'm not sure I can move or even think right

now," he said the moment his thoughts came back into focus.

"You don't need to do either because I hope you're not expecting me to move in any kind of way. That was incredible. I think I could actually feel the world spinning."

Brandon didn't move, but he kissed her face and her neck and knew that he would never again have his wife feeling like she wasn't enough for him. She was more than enough and they were meant for each other.

"I felt it, too and that was one of the best experiences I've ever had. My body wasn't my own," he admitted.

"That's because we were one and our bodies belong to each other," she said.

Brandon lifted up and looked right in her eyes.

"I love you so much and this weekend isn't just about rekindling because I don't think we really lost anything. I just needed to focus as much time on my relationship with you and the kids as I do on work. What we may see as reconnecting will just be our normal way of interacting every day. I don't want our love to be something that we have to work for. I want it to be as natural as breathing."

Dakota caressed his face, wiping a sheen of perspiration that had formed across his forehead.

"I'm right here with you, baby," she said.

"You know, we didn't get to dessert. We have fresh fruit, all kinds of pastries and we have all that chocolate in front of the fireplace waiting for us."

"Well, unless you plan on bringing all of that into this room and on this bed, I'm not sure my legs are working right now," Dakota admitted.

Brandon laughed knowing he was ravenous in his appetite for her.

"Well, if you don't stop being this sexy, you may never walk again, at least for this weekend," he joked.

"You know that means you'll have to carry me everywhere."

"Baby, I will carry you anywhere you need to go."

"For now, why don't you get us some fruit and some of those chocolates because I think I'm going to need the energy."

Brandon kissed her and then slipped off the bed.

"Would you like anything else while I'm getting up?" he asked.

Dakota looked at him like a woman crazed for more of what they'd just experienced.

"Yes, didn't you say there was whipped cream? I have a special need for that," she said and laughed when Brandon moved even faster to oblige.

13 Love on Top
4 months later

"So, Christmas in Colorado?" Alisha asked.

"Yes! Aren't you excited? Brandon put this trip together without any help from me. He has been keeping his travel agent busy."

Dakota could barely contain her excitement as she continued laying out Jasmine and Braden's clothes along with Alisha, for their family trip to Colorado Springs for the holiday.

"I am and I can't believe he was able to get my parents out of Virginia and in the freezing cold, snow covered mountains of Colorado. Is your family coming, too?"

"I was shocked when he told me my mother and brother and his family are coming along. This is going to be a fun time skiing, bowling, skating and having great family fun around the nightly fireplace."

"Yeah, well no skiing for you. My niece or

nephew that's brewing in your belly hasn't agreed to anytime on the slopes, so don't even think about it. I'm looking forward to this next baby you're about to have for me," Alisha laughed.

At the mention of the fact that she was pregnant, Dakota reached down and rubbed her small growing belly. At four months, she was a little bigger than she'd been with Jasmine and Braden and that was because she and Brandon were holding on to the secret that she was carrying twins and not just one baby. They were planning on telling the family about it once everyone arrived in Colorado.

"Trust me, I don't plan on doing a lot of anything besides relaxing. Brandon told me he plans on making sure I barely lift a finger the whole time, sort of what he does now."

"I'm happy to hear that things turned around for the better for you and my brother. I was really worried that I would have to fight the two of you for custody of my niece and nephew because if you hadn't worked it out, I was going to resolve that neither of you deserved those kids you had for me," Alisha laughed

Dakota threw a pillow at her from the bed and joined her in laughter.

"Things definitely turned around after that magical weekend we spent at *The Fisher Island Club*. Then we took the kids to Disney that next week and had the time of our lives and not once did he handle any business. I wish I could tell you about the hot weekend we spent in Belize while the kids were with your parents in Virginia. If I told you, I'd have to kill you," she joked.

"I don't need to know and I'm assuming that's when the new baby was conceived. Y'all are so nasty, always doing it all over the place."

"That's what we do and speaking of doing it all over the place, how is Chris? Is he coming to Colorado?"

"He's coming in one day after everyone else. He has a case that he's wrapping up in court and then he'll join us."

"I'm glad things are working out with him. Maybe one day before I'm old and gray, you'll give me a niece or nephew to spoil like you do my kids. I want you to see how it feels," she laughed.

"Trust me, you'll be the second to know. I'm glad Brandon has finally learned how to balance home and work better. Since he and Aiden made me an equal partner in the supper clubs, they don't get involved in those anymore and I have taken total control over running those and that has freed up a lot of both of their time. I think what really helped was the extra managers and other staff they hired to take the load off of them. Aiden has stepped his game up more so that Brandon could focus on you and the kids."

"Your brother has done more than he said he would. He has definitely put his love for me and the kids on top of everything else. I've also learned to let him focus on work when he really needs to be on top of that. We're both learning to balance our expectations for each other. He has done so much apologizing and I had a lot of apologizing to do myself for making him feel like he had to choose between me and the kids and his drive to be successful. I became selfish and blamed him for everything and that was wrong. Since we took the time to talk things through and agreed to work on being more understanding of each other, things are wonderful."

"That growing belly of yours is a testament. I know you both wanted more children, but with the problems you were having, I didn't know if you'd ever get back on the same page when it came to more children."

"Well, this bundle here was a total surprise, but a wonderful one. I've always wanted more children, but after business really started taking off for Brandon, I wasn't sure he wanted anymore. He was happier about the pregnancy than I was and he's been doing everything he can to be more of a presence at home. The kids are happier, I'm happier and he is most definitely happier, just in case you haven't noticed."

Alisha smirked at her.

"Girl, the world has noticed my brother walking around on clouds."

"Anybody here!"

Alisha and Dakota jumped at hearing Brandon holler up to them.

"We're in the bedroom," Dakota hollered back.

They turned when Brandon appeared in the doorway. As if no one besides he and Dakota were in the room, Alisha watched him walk over and without exchanging any words, pulled his wife into his arms, capturing a kiss that every woman wished she could be greeted with when her man enters a room.

"I guess I should excuse myself. I'll go pick up Jasmine from her ice skating lesson and I'll leave you to whatever is about to happen here," she joked.

Brandon didn't even look her way to respond.

"Yeah, I suggest you make an exit that breaks the sound barrier. I know you don't want to be a witness to what's about to happen within these walls!"

"Bye, Alisha," Dakota said, rushing her out.

"Y'all are so nasty."

"Well, it's about to get nastier and that's your last warning," Brandon said, laughing.

"Yeah, I'm leaving."

"These clothes are covering the area on the bed where I need you to be under me in the next few minutes," he uttered and Dakota was more than ready. Her hormones were out of control and she was thankful that Brandon always knew when she needed him.

The sexy tone of his deep, sexy voice made her shiver and her desire for wanting all of him amped up knowing they were home alone and anything goes when they are home alone. The hair on her arms tickled the moment she felt his lips caress her neck and her sex jumped as he kissed his way down her chest, unbuttoning her top as he did so. The moment her breasts were more exposed to his liking, it was mere seconds when she felt her top and her bra that he'd unsnapped with a quick flick of his fingers, dropped to the floor.

"What's got you in this mood?" she asked, helping to move things along quicker by reaching down for his belt and zipper which he quickly did away with and backed them closer to the bed.

"Anytime I think of you I'm in this mood. How are you and my growing babies doing?" he asked swiping the clothes to the floor, lifting her and laying her flat on her back. Wasting no time discarding the rest of his clothes and divesting her of the jeans and panties that were keeping him from that part of her that had him speeding through traffic to get to her, he moved against her showing what was coming next.

"Growing like weeds because all they want me to do is eat all the time. I'm going to be fat catering to their appetite and mine."

"Fat is good baby and I will still love and adore every single inch of you."

Before she could respond, Brandon slid her

behind to the edge of the bed, spread her legs over his shoulder and licked a path from her inner thigh to the sweet spot that was his pot of gold. The moment Dakota sighed her pleasure, he went in deeper and added suction to his ministration.

"Ahh...you are so good at that!" Dakota moaned as her hips moved in a little grinding motion as his tongue continued to titillate her.

"I know what my baby loves and what her body needs," he hummed.

Going back to making this moment about her, he didn't let up until her hips practically lifted off of the bed and when she screamed his name he applied the right amount of pressure with his tongue and he felt her fly apart into a million pieces as she shattered with pleasure over and over again. Before letting her come completely down from her sensual high, he stood and breathing in deeply, taking in some of the intoxicatingly delightful carnal haze that engulfed them, he spread her legs and while taking her lips in a searing kiss the continued to flame his desire for her, he entered her body in one long swoop as he pushed in to the hilt, causing him to expel all of the air in his lungs.

The way her body was gripping his hardness, he felt like a crazed man and he surged into her while holding her legs up, over his shoulders.

"You feel so good. Let me know if your legs are uncomfortable," he said, breathlessly while trying to control the urge to pump relentlessly into her.

"You always make me feel good and right now is no exception and my legs are fine, so don't you dare hold back!"

"I love you!" he shouted and gave them both what they loved about making love together.

Using power strokes, he stoked the fire that was burning in his body for the only woman who could make him feel this way. Hearing her moans and encouraging him to give her more, he gave her everything he knew she wanted and needed. The minute Dakota raised her hips to meet thrusts, he knew he wouldn't be able to hold on much longer and there was no greater feeling than to experience his release with the love of his life.

Reaching down between them, he wanted to see and feel her as she raced toward her second mighty orgasm. The moment his fingers encountered that hard nub above the entrance to where her body continued to grip him tight, he knew she'd be there and he was right there with her. On the scream of his name from her lips, Brandon let go as his body exploded along with hers and he rode out the passionate moment on a high that he never, ever wanted to come down from.

Slowing the gyration of his hips, he leaned up to look into the face of the woman who was his everything. Moving them further up on the bed to a more comfortable position, he moved to the side and turned them in a way that they were facing each other.

"Thank you for never giving up on my love for you. I have been happy with our love since the first day I laid eyes on you. I never want you to ever again question or doubt what you mean to me. I wouldn't survive without your love. I wouldn't make it if I didn't have you to come home to and love me the way you do. I couldn't wait to get through that door, run up these steps to make love to you. I couldn't think of anything or focus on anything, but you today and that's how I want every day to be. I know that work will interfere sometimes, but it will never take the place of me putting my love for you and our family on top of everything else going on in my life. Without you, I am nothing. I love you, baby."

Brandon said a quiet thank you as Dakota reached over and caressed his face and he saw the signs of unshed tears in her eyes.

"Thank you for my love on top! I love you so much and though I don't believe in everything in life being perfect, I believe in our perfect love and that's the kind of love that I will fight forever to hold on to. You, Jasmine, Braden and these two little one's I'm carrying are a true testament that nothing about our life should ever be taken for granted. Thank you for always putting your love for us first!"

"Are you ready for a fun family vacation in wintery Colorado? I can't wait to sit around the fireplace with our family and have great fun."

"I can't believe everyone is going, including Aiden and Alisha. Who's going to take care of business while you're all away?" she asked.

"For the most part, we've given everyone time off for the holiday, so while we're spending time with family, I wanted our teams to be able to do the same thing. There will be no work until after the new year and I don't plan to do anything work related. The nightclub team is ready for our busy holiday season, especially New Year's Eve and I trust that they can handle things while we're away. Unless there is an emergency, I've instituted the same warning to everyone, that I am not to be disturbed. I have others in place to handle anything work related that can't wait until after the holiday. This time is about family and I'm looking forward to getting my kids on skis on the slopes."

Dakota looked at him with a warning on her face.

"Baby slopes, please. I know our kids are daredevils like you are, but I don't think I can handle it since I can't be out there with them."

"Okay, I promise no big slopes, yet, but I don't want our kids afraid to enjoy the kind of life we can provide for them and that means trips like this one to Colorado. I think we should get up before Alisha and Jasmine get here. Aiden has Braden with him and I don't think they're coming back anytime soon."

As they moved and stood up, Dakota walked

toward the bathroom with him watching her every move.

"I love the way you move!" he exclaimed.

He watched as she turned her head toward him slowly with a "come-here because I have something for you" kind of look.

"Want to see how I move in the shower?" she asked, ravenous for more of him.

"You don't have to ask me twice," Brandon said and raced to join her.

Get books 1 – 4 of the Bachelor Series

Book 1 – "Bachelor Not for Sale"
Now available

Even self-proclaimed "bachelors for life" meet that one woman that makes them want to slow down and second guess bachelorhood. After suffering through the heartache of what he thought was true love, Duron Knight meets and becomes enchanted with bombshell Taija Charles.

Taija has heard a lot about Duron and all of her body senses are on overdrive when she meets the handsome bachelor face to face. As the sparks fly, Taija plans to show Duron how she can help him mend his broken heart with real love and the right amount of lust.

Book 2 – "A Designed Affair"
Now available

In the follow-up to "Bachelor Not for Sale", Loren Knight has been engaging in a secret love affair with her brother Duron's best friend and business partner, Michael Bailey. He is everything she could want and more in a man, but she believes the risk is too great for any type of relationship with him beyond the bedroom door.

Michael Bailey has been fighting his attraction to Loren for years. He has stayed away from her out of respect for his best friend and business partner. Now that he and Loren have finally given into passion that they both have been craving, can Michael convince Loren that what they share is worth the risk?

Book 3 – "A Perfect Combination
Now available

In the third installment following "Bachelor Not for Sale" and "A Designed Affair", Tyrone Davis is the king of one-night-stands; nicknamed, *Mr. Love Them and Leave Them*. He learned to perfect it from his two best friends, Duron Knight and Michael Bailey. He never imagined a one-night stand would have such a lasting impact, but that's exactly what happened.

Victoria Alston couldn't forget the incredible night she spent with Tyrone Davis, someone connected to one of her best friends. The next day, she disappeared, returning to reality and the fiancé she'd left in Boston while on business travel. They both soon discovered that it wasn't just a one-night stand, but a perfect combination for love.

Book 4 – "Love at Last"
Now available

They had the perfect love...That's what Brian Knight thought of his relationship with Sherry Braxton until he looked up one day and she was gone and never wanted to see him again. Two years later, he discovered that there is the possibility that Sherry may have been pregnant with his child. Hurt and angry at her deceit, he takes a flight to Baltimore to fight for his rights as a father and realizes that the love and passion they once shared had never died. Is it possible he could still have the kind of love he thought would last a lifetime? Can he still have his love at last?

From Cheryl Barton – "Un-Break My Heart"
Now Available

Dr. Mackenzie Ellis suffered a loss so great, she never thought she'd fall in love again, especially with someone close to her.

Travis Blackwell, III never dreamed of crossing the line with Mackenzie until his heart would no longer allow him to deny the love he has for her and the passion he wants to share with her knowing that he is the key to mending her broken heart.

From Cheryl Barton – "Bossy"
Now Available

Cassidy 'Bossy' Bostic came from nothing, but knew she would be something. Pregnant and alone, she was forced to run from her past in order to have a future. Her rise to the top as the owner of a fashion dynasty is what dreams are made of, but her hard, icy persona could have her living a lonely existence.

Drake Montgomery, a rising attorney heading toward the political arena, has fallen in love with the 'Bossy' mogul only to discover it's 'Cassidy' he loves, but 'Bossy', not so much.

Can their hot, steamy romance melt even her cold, icy heart? Only time and love will tell.

From Cheryl Barton – "Heartthrob"
Now Available

Cade Weston, Hollywood's most eligible bachelor and named the world's sexiest man of the year, lives life at the top with a bevy of beauties at his beck and call, people providing his every desire and more money than any one person should have.

Callie Hurston struggles to make it as a stylist to the stars in a world where women are intimidated by her beauty and men are interested in her body and not her talent.

Cade thought he had it all until he has a chance meeting with Callie and decides to take a chance on her talent and ends up taking an even bigger chance with his heart.

Can the playboy turn in his player's card and give in to love?

From Cheryl Barton – "His Halloween Promise"
Now Available

Dylan Kennedy and Savannah Eaton-Kennedy may be divorced, but that doesn't stop them from indulging in some pretty hot and sexy encounters.

A divorce decree may mean that their life together is over, but Dylan has a promise to keep that could bring his wife back where she belongs; in his life, permanently.

From Cheryl Barton – "Home for Thanksgiving"
Now Available

Firefighter Nicholas Sullivan is going home for the holiday after he was sidelined due to an injury on the job. Guilt over a life lost has kept him away from his family's ranch in Montana and now he's forced to face his past demons and deal with a self-imposed life of regret.

Veterinarian Parker Wingate's first encounter with the handsome firefighter was less than pleasurable. She sympathized with his hurt, understood his pain and before long, felt his love.

Knowing the holiday season is ending soon, can Nick go from living in love for the moment to allowing himself to finally live in love forever?

From Cheryl Barton – "A Better Man"
Now Available

Phoenix Graham is living her best life with the best man, her fiancé, Carson Stone, heir to the Stone Tower Hotel Empire. Her perfect life is shaken up when a handsome, rugged and extremely sexy mysterious man moves in across the hall and she begins to see that the rose-colored glasses she had been seeing life through were blinders. She soon discovers that Carson was the best man for her until she takes notice of a better man and his name is Gavin Black.

What's a girl to do when the best doesn't get better and better is what she craves?

From Cheryl Barton
Book 5 of the "Amorous Occupations" series
"The Electrician" – Now Available

The party invitation said everyone had to wear a masquerade mask the entire night, a New Orleans tradition. Dara Marshall couldn't resist the opportunity to spend an uninhibited night of passion with National Football Association coach

Nelson Riley, the guest of honor, knowing that her identity was hidden by her mask.

Dara's world turns upside down when she discovers the gorgeous coach is the newest client of her father's business and after she's sent on a job at his condo, she does everything in her power to not give away the secret of who she is.

Nelson could never forget the sexy temptress he'd spent an unforgettable night with, even when she tries to hide behind a mask and baggy overalls.

About the Author

Cheryl Barton lives in Maryland and in her spare time she loves to read espionage novels, cook, watch Sci-fi movies, spend time with family and friends and enjoy Maryland steamed crabs.

Indulge in more romance and inspirational novels by Cheryl Barton by visiting her website at www.cherylbarton.net.

I am because you read and I thank you! - *Cheryl*

Connect with me

Visit my website at www.CherylBarton.net
Twitter – @Author Cheryl Barton
Instagram – AuthorCherylBarton
Facebook at Author Cheryl Barton
Email – Cheryl@CherylBarton.net
Blog - https://mswriterinmd.wordpress.com/

www.ingramcontent.com/pod-product-compliance
Lightning Source LLC
Chambersburg PA
CBHW050820180626
46814CB00004B/1389